SNOWBALL IN HELL

JOSH LANYON

VELLICHOR BOOKS

An imprint of JustJoshin Publishing, Inc.

Snowball in Hell

Los Angeles, 1943

Just back from
the European Theater,
reporter Nathan Doyle
is asked to cover the murder
of a society blackmailer—
a man who,
Homicide Detective
Mathew Spain believes,
Nathan had every reason
to want dead.

SNOWBALL IN HELL
July 2020
Copyright (c) 2007 by Josh Lanyon
Cover and book design by Kevin Burton Smith
Edited by Keren Reed
All rights reserved

Published in the United States of America

JustJoshin Publishing, Inc.
3053 Rancho Vista Blvd.
Suite 116
Palmdale, CA 93551
www.joshlanyon.com

This is a work of fiction. Any resemblance to persons living or dead is entirely coincidental.

CHAPTER ONE

"**H**ell of a thing," Jonesy said for the third time.

Matt agreed. It was a hell of a thing. He turned his gaze from the gaggle of reporters smoking and talking beside the grouping of snarling cement saber-toothed tigers, and returned his attention to the sticky, bedraggled corpse currently watching the birdie for the police photographer.

Whoever had dumped the dead man had counted on the body sinking in the black ooze of the Brea Pits, and in the heat of the summer when the tar heated up and softened...maybe. But it was December, a little more than a week before Christmas, and it had been raining steadily for two days. No chance in hell. The body had rested there, facedown in the rainwater hiding the treacherous crust of tar beneath, until the museum paleontologists excavating the site for fossils had made the grisly early-morning discovery.

"Looks kinda familiar," Jonesy remarked gloomily, as the plastered hair and drowned eyes were briefly illuminated in the white flash of the camera.

Matt bit back a laugh. "Yeah? Must be the fact that he's dead."

Jonesy looked reproachful, although after thirty-three years on the homicide squad, he'd seen more than his share of stiffs. They both had, though Matt had seen more violent death and destruction during his seven months in the Pacific than he had in his eleven years on the force.

"No identification on him at all?"

"Nope. Even the label was cut out of his jacket. No sign of his hat or shoes."

Matt considered this. Soaking in water and tar hadn't done John Doe's clothes much good, and they'd have to wait 'til everything dried before they could hope to get much from an examination. How much they would get then was doubtful, but that suit didn't look particularly old or worn, and the tailoring was the kind that showed its worth even in the worst conditions—which these were.

Laughter drifted from the circle of statues where the reporters and a couple of photographers waited impatiently. Matt knew most of them: Williams from "The Peach," Mackey from the *Times*, Cohen from the *Mirror* and Tara Renee of the *Examiner*. The only one he didn't recognize was the slim man lighting Tara's cigarette. Thin, brown fingers cupped the lighter against the damp breeze; lean, tanned cheek creased in a smile as Tara flirted with him. Tara flirted with everyone, but she was a good little crime hound.

"Who's that?" Matt asked Jonesy, and Jonesy looked up from the meticulous diagrams he was making of the crime scene and followed Matt's stare.

"Doyle. *Tribune-Herald*. Heard he was with the Eighth Army in North Africa 'til he picked up a case of lead poisoning." Jonesy grinned his lopsided smile. "Got hit by machine-gun fire in Tunisia."

"Yeah, well, there's a lot of that going around." But Matt's interest was unwillingly caught. "So he's English?"

"Nah. Hometown boy, Loot."

"Doc's here, Lieutenant," one of the uniformed officers said as the police ambulance bumped its way over the grassy verge.

Matt nodded and then nodded again toward the reporters. "Tell 'em I want to see Miss Renee and..." He thought it over. "Doyle."

When he glanced back, Jonesy was giving him an old-fashioned look.

"What's that for?" He'd known Jonesy a long time; Jonesy had been Matt's old man's partner. Back then he'd been big and rawboned with a shock of red hair and a face full of freckles. The hair was gray now, and the freckles had faded into a permanently ruddy complexion, but he was still one of the best detectives on the force—sometimes Matt was afraid Jonesy was too good a detective.

"She's a firecracker, that dame. Can't understand why any woman would want the police beat."

"I guess she got tired of garden parties and ladies' fashion." He watched the uni approach the reporters. Heard the protests of the men from the *Daily News,* the *Times* and the *Mirror.* Watched Doyle's surprise at the summons. Doyle looked past the officer and caught Matt's gaze. Matt held it for a moment, then looked away, jotting down a few more crime scene details in his notebook. From the tire tracks, it looked like whoever dumped Mr. Doe into the goo had driven as close as he safely could to the water's edge. Maybe that meant something, maybe not.

Out of the corner of his eye Matt could see Tara and Doyle crossing the soggy grass toward him. Tara's heels sank into the mud, and Doyle cupped a chivalrous hand beneath her elbow, which amused Matt in a sour way. Tara either had designs on Doyle or thought she could get something out of him—anyone else would have been handed his arm back half-chewed.

"Doesn't look like he drowned," Jonesy was saying.

"He didn't drown," Matt replied.

The police ambulance rolled to a stop and parked in the weeds and mud. Across the field and through the trees

Matt could see oil derricks slowly bowing and scraping against the leaden sky.

"What a smell!" Matt heard Tara exclaim, and the other reporter, Doyle, said, "Bitumen." He had a quiet voice, and Matt only caught his reply because he was listening for it.

"Hello, Lieutenant," Tara said, and Matt turned to face her. "To what do we owe this honor?" Tara was a very pretty girl with glossy black curls, sparkling dark eyes, rosy cheeks and a little pointed chin that she wagged too much. But somehow Matt didn't like to shut her up. Maybe because she reminded him a little of Rachel.

"Miss Renee," he said gravely. He glanced at her companion. "You're Doyle from the *Tribune-Herald?*"

"That's right." Beneath the khaki trench coat, Doyle was medium height and very thin. His hair, what Matt could see of it beneath his wide-brimmed hat, was very fair—sun bleached. He had the overlay of tan that comes from years spent under a blazing sun, but beneath it he was sallow. His eyes were light, maybe blue, maybe gray—unexpectedly bright in his lean face. He studied Matt curiously.

"We've got a little problem," Matt said to Tara. "I thought you might be able to help." She gave him a pert, inquiring look, and Matt stepped aside so they could get a look at John Doe. "Either of you recognize him?"

He was watching Doyle. Not because he expected Doyle to recognize the dead guy—he didn't figure Doyle had been back in town long enough to be of much use there—he was just giving him a break after Tunisia. Doyle glanced down at the corpse with the weary indifference of a man who's seen too much death—and froze.

There wasn't any mistake. Doyle's blue-gray eyes widened. He went perfectly still, apparently forgetting to breathe.

Next to him, Tara gasped, and Matt automatically turned his attention, thinking a drowned man was too much for her first thing after breakfast. "Phil Arlen," she murmured. She raised her dark eyes. "That's Philip Arlen."

Jonesy gave a low whistle.

Matt asked, "Benedict Arlen's kid?"

"I'm sure of it."

Matt could feel the echo of her words rippling through the ranks of the crime-scene men. Benedict Arlen was old money, oil money.

Matt looked back at Doyle, but Doyle had recovered himself. He met Matt's gaze and agreed evenly, "It's Arlen."

"You knew him?"

"I went to school with Bob. His brother. Robert Arlen."

"The old school tie," Matt said dryly. "Was that high school or college?"

"Loyola High School. Loyola University."

Catholic, Matt thought. Jesuit trained. Not that it mattered to him. He hadn't given a damn before the war, and he sure as hell thought the world should have learned something about hate by now.

The coroner joined their little tableau. Doc Mason was a beanpole of a man in a black raincoat. As usual, he was smoking a pipe, the pleasant homely scent carried on the rainswept breeze helping to mask other, less pleasant, odors. "Okay for me to get to work, Lieutenant?"

"He's all yours," Matt said. "The crime scene was contaminated from the minute the professors pulled him out of the drink."

Doyle was watching him with those light, alert eyes.

"What a scoop!" Tara said. "And here I thought it was a slow week for news."

"When was the last time you saw Phil Arlen?" Matt asked Doyle.

Doyle shrugged. "It's been a while."

"Nathan's only been home a couple of weeks," Tara said. "He was a war correspondent in North Africa. He was wounded at Medenine." She made it sound like Doyle had done something especially clever. Yep, she was interested in Doyle all right.

At the same time Matt could feel Doyle's discomfort, his desire to shut Tara up. Matt could have told him to save his strength.

"Had enough for one war?" he asked, not unsympathetically.

"So they tell me," Doyle said.

"Lieutenant Spain was on Guadalcanal," Tara put in ruthlessly. "He took two bullets in the leg."

"Now I can predict rain." Matt held out his hand as a fat drop hit his nose, and Doyle laughed. He had an easy, rather husky laugh. Matt found himself smiling back, but he wasn't forgetting Doyle's shocked reaction to the body of Phil Arlen. Of course that could have been the jolt of a John Doe turning out to be someone he knew—but if he instantly recognized Phil Arlen waterlogged and streaked in mud and tar, he must have seen him fairly recently. And as far as Matt knew, the closest Arlen had come to the front lines was watching newsreels in the front row of Grauman's.

"Have you found any shells?" Doyle asked, watching the coroner. Tara did a double take.

"You've got sharp eyes," Matt commented. And now Doyle had attracted Jonesy's attention too.

"He was shot?" Tara asked.

"He was shot all right," Doc Mason said, getting to his feet. "Twenty-two caliber maybe, fairly close range. Must have hit the sternum and ricocheted around inside. There's no exit wound." He chewed on his pipe stem. "Something funny here."

Aware of two very quiet and very attentive reporters, Matt said, "Fill me in later."

Doc nodded. "We better get him inside."

The rain began to patter down as a couple of men lifted Arlen's body onto a stretcher and carried him across the grass to the waiting ambulance. The morning smelled of rain and asphalt and pipe tobacco.

A couple of yards away, the other reporters had moved from grumbling to outright sedition.

"Okay, thanks for your help." Matt nodded dismissal to Nathan Doyle and Tara.

"You're not making a statement?" Doyle asked.

"Lieutenant Spain never allows himself to be rushed," Tara informed him, and Matt shook his head a little at her.

His eyes met Doyle's again, and a smile tugged at Doyle's mouth.

"Welcome to the neighborhood, Mr. Doyle," Matt said.

"Thanks." Despite the smile, there was a shadowy look to Doyle's eyes, the kind of fatigue that didn't have anything to do with lack of sleep or months in a hospital. There was no question which beat Doyle would have preferred to be covering.

"Come on," Tara said, and she linked her arm in Doyle's. "The royal audience is at an end."

Sardonically, Matt watched her shepherd Doyle, the two of them hoofing straight for the main gate, skirting their clustered colleagues who threw friendly and not-so-friendly jeers and insults after them. Lights flashing, the coroner's ambulance rumbled past them, splashing through the pools of muddy water as it turned the opposite way, heading for the rear entrance of the park.

"That Doyle's an interesting fella," Jonesy remarked.

Matt said nothing, turning back to face the silvery-black pool.

He and Jonesy just stood there. Matt was thinking about the unpleasant task before him: informing Benedict Arlen that his youngest child was dead. Kind of ironic when everyone knew Arlen had paid a small fortune to keep the kid out of the draft. And now he was dead. Murdered. He might have had a better chance dodging bullets overseas.

As he watched, a giant bubble of methane gas formed on the watery surface of the pit, expanded and dissipated in a silent gooey pop.

"Disrespectful, tossing the Arlen kid in that muck," Jonesy said reflectively.

"Homicide's disrespectful," Matt replied.

Benedict Arlen lived in a white stucco Spanish colonial revival-style mansion in Mandeville Canyon. The house was surrounded by twenty acres of palm trees and hedges and flowering Mediterranean plants. Two bison, clearly pets, ambled contently past the large tiled fountains.

A butler who must have been dragged out of retirement—or possibly eternity—when the regular guy enlisted, met them at the carved wooden doors and did his unsteady best to run interference.

Matt left Jonesy to deal with the majordomo, and he proceeded along the tiled hallway lined with paintings of the Old West by Charlie Russell, until he came to a room and heard voices behind a half-open door.

"You're wrong, Nathan," a man was saying in a querulous voice. "I tell you, Philip is perfectly all right."

Matt couldn't hear the answer, just the quiet murmur of words, but he had the disquieted feeling he knew that voice. He pushed open the door onto a room with a Gothic ceiling and leaded windows with iron grilles. There were vibrant Indian rugs on the floor and lots of heavy, dark

Spanish furniture. Oil paintings by Frederic Remington decorated the white walls, and bronze sculptures of bronco busters and buffalo hunters topped the tables.

Benedict Arlen sat on a long velvet covered sofa next to a giant fireplace in natural stone. A captain-of-industry portrait of him hung over the fireplace—he didn't do it justice. He was a frail-looking man in a plum-colored smoking jacket. He had a beaky nose and thin white hair.

Standing in front of the fireplace was Nathan Doyle.

He glanced up as Matt entered the room, and his expression was unreadable. He said coolly, "Lieutenant Spain, isn't it?"

"It was three hours ago. I'd be hurt if you'd forgotten already."

Doyle said, "I haven't forgotten."

"What are you doing here?" Matt figured he knew what Doyle was doing there. He'd known a few news hawks like that, willing to do anything, pushing past the women and children, trampling over flowerbeds and graves to be first with a story, but he hadn't thought Doyle was the type.

Studying him now—slim and self-contained as he warmed himself in front of Benedict Arlen's cavern-sized fireplace—he still didn't seem like the type.

And Matt thought again about Doyle's recoil when he recognized Phil Arlen's body.

Maybe he'd been shocked because he didn't expect to see Arlen's body there because…that wasn't where he'd left it.

When you're a cop you learn to think like that.

Jonesy slipped quietly into the room behind Matt. He took out his pad and pencil. Doyle opened his mouth to respond to Matt's question, but Benedict Arlen beat him to the punch.

"What is the meaning of this?" he demanded, like somebody in a play. He sat bolt upright, staring from Matt to Doyle as though he suspected they might be in this—whatever it was—together. Which was certainly an odd idea.

Matt identified himself with a show of his badge, and Arlen goggled as though he couldn't believe it.

Doyle said, "I thought Mr. Arlen should hear about Phil from someone besides the police. That it would be less of a shock."

"I tell you Philip is perfectly all right," the old man protested, but now he sounded frightened. "We've paid the ransom. There's no reason for them to harm him."

It was obvious from Doyle's expression that this information was news to him. He stared at Arlen, and Matt said, "Sir, are you telling me that your son was kidnapped?"

The old man hesitated, chewing his lip. "We received a call Sunday evening informing us that Philip had been… taken. We were given twenty-four hours to deliver one hundred thousand dollars."

The old man faltered as Jonesy whistled. "We were promised that Philip would be released twenty-four hours after that." At Matt's expression he said defiantly, "We didn't inform the police. We were expressly ordered *not* to inform the police or Philip's life would be forfeit."

Doyle rubbed his forehead and said nothing. He didn't look at Benedict or Matt.

Matt said, "I'm very sorry to inform you, Mr. Benedict, but Phil was found shot to death this morning at Brea Tar Pits."

The old man shook his head stubbornly.

Everyone's initial reaction was denial; Matt had been through this too many times to count. There was nothing for it but the straight truth. He drove on. "His body was recovered by some of the museum staff members working at the dig. Mr. Doyle made the initial identification, but we'll need confirmation."

The door to the room opened and a tall, elegant woman strode into the room. She wore trousers—the kind that only certain rich, fashionable ladies wore—and her dark hair was coiled intricately on her head. "Dad, they're saying on the radio that Phil is *dead*." She stopped short, taking in Doyle's presence. "Nathan..." She looked at Matt. "So it's true."

"Yes," Nathan said. "I'm sorry, Ronnie."

"Lieutenant Spain, Homicide Division," Matt said. "And you are—?"

"Veronica Thompson-Arlen," she said. "I'm married to Robert Arlen, Phil's brother." She glanced at the old man sitting bent forward, head in hands, and she slipped past Matt and sat beside him on the sofa, putting an arm around his shoulder. "Oh, Dad. I don't know what to say."

She looked up at Nathan. "Couldn't there be any mistake?"

Nathan shook his head. "It's Phil."

Matt said, "What do you know about this kidnapping?"

She barely glanced his way. "Not a lot. Bob, my husband, was supposed to deliver the ransom money on Monday night to the Griffith Park Observatory. He did. Everything went according to clockwork on our end." She shook her head. "I can't understand why they would have killed him."

"They?" Nathan asked. He caught Matt's eye and looked momentarily discomfited.

"I—I just assume there would be more than one of them. A gang, perhaps. It was a woman's voice on the telephone both times. But a woman wouldn't have been able to kidnap Phil without help of some kind, surely?"

"Both times?" Matt repeated, with an eye to Doyle.

"A woman called Sunday evening to tell us Phil had been kidnapped and that we had twenty-four hours to gather the ransom money. Then Monday evening she called and told us where to deliver the money. She promised that Phil would be released unharmed Tuesday, this evening—if everything went according to plan."

"And the money was left at the Griffith Park Observatory? Inside or out?"

"Outside. The planetarium is only open in the day now to prevent enemy planes from using its lights to target the city. The money was to be put in a satchel and placed on the east observation terrace in a planter beside a little staircase leading to an arched doorway. Bob was supposed to leave the money and walk away—which he did." She turned back to the old man. "He did everything they wanted, Dad. You know that."

The old man said nothing.

"We'll need to talk to your husband, Mrs. Arlen."

"Thompson-Arlen. Yes, of course. He's at home today. He wanted to be available…in case."

Matt nodded thoughtfully, studying Benedict Arlen. The old man seemed to have retreated into his own dazed thoughts.

He glanced at Doyle. He was watching the old man and the woman without emotion. The fireplace threw shadows across his thin face. Made his eyes glint oddly.

"Again, very sorry for your loss," Matt said formally. "We'll keep you informed as the investigation develops."

Neither the man nor the woman responded. Matt looked at Doyle again, and found him watching him. He said shortly, "Did you want to tag along to Robert Arlen's?"

"Sure." Doyle's surprise was evident.

Matt said, "Come on, then. You can introduce us." He was thinking it might be a good idea to keep an eye on Mr. Doyle of the *Tribune-Herald*.

"Why would they have killed him?" Doyle sounded like he was thinking aloud. Matt glanced his way, and Doyle glanced back. He seemed genuinely puzzled. "If the ransom was paid, why did they kill Phil?"

"I don't know. It's not good business," Matt admitted. He was very conscious of Doyle sitting a few inches from him. Very conscious of his restless energy, of the faint, heathery aftershave he wore, of the fact that Doyle was as physically aware of him as he was of Doyle. He could tell from the way Doyle avoided even the most casual physical contact, and from those flickery sideways looks he was giving him.

"They should have called us at the start," Jonesy said. "They made a big mistake not calling us in."

"It doesn't make sense," Doyle said. "They have to realize that no one else will pay a ransom if there's no chance of getting the kidnap victim back alive."

"They may not be professionals," Matt said. "This may have been a one time only."

Doyle thought this over. "True."

"Hell of a time for this," Jonesy said. "Christmas." He shook his head.

Matt spoke to Doyle. "What were you doing at the Arlen house?"

Doyle turned those cool, lake-water eyes his way. "I told you. I thought the old man should have fair warning before you lot turned up."

"Us lot?" Matt said. Every so often Doyle had—not an accent, exactly, but an English turn of phrase. It sort of irritated Matt—and it sort of amused him. The more he saw of Nathan Doyle, the more interested he was. Mostly it was professional interest. Mostly. He said, "Now why don't I believe that?"

Doyle stared. "I don't know. It's the truth."

And now Matt was convinced it wasn't. Maybe Doyle read that in his expression. He said, "All right, honestly, I'm not sure. I did think the news would come better from someone who wasn't a cop. But...maybe it was also curiosity. Reporter's instinct."

Jonesy met Matt's eyes in the rearview mirror. Matt asked, "Did you know about the kidnapping?"

"No." Doyle was definite, and Matt thought he believed him—on that point.

"What was Philip Arlen like?"

"I didn't know him well."

"Yeah, you said. You're pals with the brother. Robert Arlen."

"We aren't pals," Doyle said. "We travel in different circles, but I knew Bob pretty well when we were at school. Phil was younger than us. I think there were about eight years between him and Bob. To tell the truth, he was a pain in the ass. The old man spoilt him rotten. I don't know how he turned out, but when he was a kid he was a tattletale and a sissy." He met Matt's gaze. "I didn't like him much."

"You're kidding."

Doyle smiled—a quirky smile that creased his lean cheek and tilted his eyes. A very attractive smile. Matt ignored it.

"When was the last time you saw him?" Matt had asked this at the tar pit. He waited to hear what Doyle would say now that he'd had time to think about it.

Doyle said vaguely, "I've seen him a couple of times at the Las Palmas Club. I can't tell you for sure."

"Okay." Doyle was too smart to tell an outright lie, but Matt was beginning to get the picture.

"How did the Brothers Arlen get along?"

Doyle's hesitation was noticeable. "Okay, I think. Phil was always the old man's favorite. I guess Bob had plenty of time to get used to the idea."

They didn't talk much after that, listening to the police radio, and the hiss of tires on wet streets.

Jonesy pulled onto Wilshire Boulevard, and they could see the neon sign of the Bryson Apartment Hotel from blocks away, burning bright in the gloomy late morning. The slick and crowded streets were decked in gaudy garland banners, palm trees twined with Christmas lights, and department store windows decorated with elaborate displays of Santa's villages and winter wonderlands.

Jonesy pulled up in front of the Bryson Apartment Hotel, and they got out, pulling hats down and collars up against the gray rain and ducking between the classical columns with their irritable-looking stone lions balanced aloft.

The Arlens lived in a penthouse on the ninth floor, below the ballroom and the glass-enclosed loggias with their distant view of Catalina Island.

Bob Arlen opened the door, took an awkward step back, steadying himself with a walking stick. He was a tall, well-built man with light brown hair. The left half of his face was badly scarred, twisting into unidentifiable emotion; the right half of his face merely looked surprised.

"Nathan," he said. "I wasn't expecting you."

"Mr. Arlen." Matt showed his badge. "Lieutenant Spain, LAPD Homicide Division. May we come in?"

He gripped his walking stick with both hands, leaning heavily on it. "It's about Phil, isn't it?"

"Yes," Nathan said. "I'm sorry, Bob."

"I read it in this morning's extra." Bob Arlen led them through to a living room with glass doors looking out onto a small balcony. Rain bounced down on large potted plants and metal railings. "I couldn't believe it. I still can't."

"We're very sorry for your loss, Mr. Arlen," Matt said formally. "You didn't go into your office today?"

"I was waiting to hear—I thought there might be news."

And there had been, though maybe not the news Arlen had been waiting for. He looked tired and shocked, but not overcome with grief. Not as far as Matt could tell.

Arlen waved them over to chairs and made his way to a rosewood bar cart laden with crystal bottles and stemware. "Can I offer you gentlemen a drink?"

"No thanks," Matt said.

"Nathan?"

"Yes, thanks, Bob."

Arlen poured two stiff whiskies from a bottle of Lord Calvert with a steady hand, although it was clearly not his first drink. "Ice? Soda?"

"Neat." Nathan took the glass with a murmur of thanks. Matt realized he was far too aware of every move Nathan Doyle made. He wanted to think it was his copper's instinct warning him, but he had the uneasy feeling it was something very different.

Bob Arlen made his way over to a low sofa, managing to juggle both his walking stick and glass with an unbeautiful efficiency that indicated a lot of practice.

"What can you tell us about your brother's kidnapping?"

Arlen sipped his whisky before his measured answer. "The *pater* got the call Sunday evening. A woman said that Phil was being held for one hundred thousand dollars, and that if we didn't come up with the money by five o'clock on Monday evening, he would be killed. She said she would call back on Monday with directions on how the ransom would be delivered."

"Any idea who this woman might have been? Was the voice familiar?"

"No."

"How long had your brother been missing at that point?"

Bob shook his head. "I wouldn't know. I'm not sure Claire would even know. Phil…came and went as he pleased. I think he spent more time at the Las Palmas Club than he did at home."

Matt looked at Nathan who said, "Claire is Phil's wife."

"They've been married just over a year," Bob said. "Claire's a sweet girl. Not really Phil's type. My father pushed for the marriage. I have no idea why."

Matt talked and let Jonesy take the notes; he'd found people talked more easily when they didn't realize they were going on the record. "And this unknown woman called back on Monday evening and told you where to deliver the money?"

"Griffith Park Observatory. It's closed at nights now, and I was supposed to leave the money in a bag in a planter on the east terrace at midnight."

"Were you on time?"

"I was early. I left the money at eleven thirty in one of the cement planters along the wall. When I came back an hour later, it was gone."

"You didn't see who took the bag?"

He shook his head. "I wanted to wait around and see if I could spot the kidnapper, but my father was adamant that we not do anything to endanger getting Phil back safely." He shrugged. "I drove away, walked around the park, looked at the merry-go-round, then went back to make sure the pick-up had been made."

Jonesy said, "Lot of things could go wrong with that plan. The fact is the kidnappers might never have received the money."

"It was their plan," Bob said. "We didn't get a vote. We had to do it their way."

Matt said, "And according to the kidnappers, if things went according to plan, your brother was to be released this evening?"

Bob nodded. "Instead, they killed him, the dirty bastards." He drained his glass, looked to see if Nathan needed a refill. Nathan did not. He was staring out the glass doors at the sparkling chains of rain.

"Did you keep a record of the numbers of the ransom money?" Matt asked.

"I wanted to. My father was against the idea."

Matt repeated patiently, "Did you keep a record?"

"Er...yes."

"Might we see that record?"

Bob left the room. A key turned in the front door lock, the door opened, and Veronica Thompson-Arlen entered. She wore a fur coat that was several years old; her cheeks were pink from the cold. Oddly enough, it seemed to Matt that when she saw them grouped around her living room, she relaxed a little.

Nodding hello, she moved over to the bar cart and poured herself a drink. She offered Nathan another. He declined, seeming to only then recall that he had a drink. He swallowed a mouthful, glanced at Matt, glanced away.

Bob returned with a list of the serial numbers.

Matt thanked him.

"What's that?" Veronica asked, and when Bob explained, she flushed. "Oh, Bob. You shouldn't have! What if the kidnappers somehow got wind of it?"

Jonesy said, "Unless they were morons, the kidnappers would assume that precaution was taken, Mrs. Arlen. Don't think for a minute keeping track of those numbers had anything to do with your brother-in-law's death."

"I hope not. Dad would be...devastated."

Matt said, "Did your brother have any enemies, Mr. Arlen?"

Bob and Veronica exchanged a funny look.

"Not that I'm aware of," Bob said.

"Oh, Bob," Veronica said wearily. "What's the point of lying?" She looked at Matt. "My brother-in-law was a charming boy, but of course he had his enemies. We all have our enemies, don't we?"

It seemed like a stagy thing to say. Matt tried to remember what, if anything, he knew about Veronica Thompson-Arlen. He thought that she had not come from money, but she acted to the manor born, so maybe he was mixing her up with the other one, Phil Arlen's wife—now widow.

"Well," he said, "I have a few, but they're mostly guys I've put behind bars. What kind of enemies did your brother-in-law have?"

"Carl Winters for one," Bob said.

"Oh, Bob!" Veronica protested, just as though she hadn't been saying a minute earlier they needed to come clean.

"Who's Carl Winters?" Once again Matt looked to Nathan Doyle for the answer. And once again Doyle knew the answer. For someone who claimed he hadn't kept in regular touch, he seemed to know a lot about the Arlens. And they seemed to still be on a first-name basis with him. Maybe it was the papal connection. The Catholic community was a tight-knit one, although Doyle didn't look like much of a churchgoer to Matt.

"Claire Arlen's brother," Doyle answered. "Her twin brother, I think. He runs a bookstore on South Grand Avenue. Rare and antiquarian books."

"I think Carl felt bitter about the way Phil treated Claire," Bob said.

"And how was that?" Matt asked.

Bob shrugged uncomfortably.

Veronica said, "Phil was not ideal husband material." She smiled at Bob, and there was no doubt she thought her own husband was a prize worth hanging on to.

"And how did Claire feel about Phil?"

There was a pause, and Veronica answered. "I guess you'd have to ask her, Lieutenant."

"I guess I will," Matt said.

Tara Renee stood frowning beneath the striped awning of the Las Palmas Club. She brightened when she spotted Matt and Jonesy. "What'd you do with Nathan?" she asked, trotting to keep up with Matt as he strode toward mahogany doors with stained-glass windows of green palm trees and azure oceans.

"Unhooked him and threw him back." Matt eyed her curiously. "What did you want me to do with him?"

"Artie Cohen said he saw you haul him off in a police car."

"We didn't haul him anywhere," Matt retorted. "We invited him to accompany us to Bob Arlen's since he knows the family. I thought he might be useful to have along."

"Was he?"

"Yep."

"Nice break for Nathan."

Matt stopped and subjected Tara to a narrow-eyed inspection. "Okay, what's on your mind, Miss Renee?"

"*Miss Renee?* You're so formal!" She dimpled at him, but Matt knew her too well to be swayed. "Nothing's on my mind. I'm glad Nathan's getting a few breaks. He deserves them. What'd you think of him?"

"What am I supposed to think of him?" Matt shrugged. "How well do you know him?"

"Are you jealous?"

He sighed.

Tara made a face. "Alright, already! Not a lot. I didn't know Nathan before the war. One thing I do know. He writes beee-ooou-ti-fully. I keep telling him he should write a novel. The kind of thing that gets slapped between embossed leather and sent to the *Saturday Evening Review* boys to chew over. He's too good for this racket."

Matt shook his head and rapped on the doors. "You seem very interested in Nathan Doyle."

"I *am* interested. He's an interesting fellow, unlike the louts I usually meet in my trade." She batted her eyelashes at Matt. "Don't worry, Lieutenant, you'll always come first with me."

"That's what worries me," Matt said, and she laughed. He liked her laugh. That was when she reminded him most of Rachel.

"Jonesy still loves me," she said, with a backward glance for Jonesy.

"You remind me of my granddaughter," Jonesy said. "She needs a good spanking too."

Tara raised her eyebrows.

Matt said, "Anyway, what the hell was he doing with the Eighth Army for how many years?"

She shrugged. "I don't know. He doesn't talk much. He did say he was in Greece in forty-one." She gave Matt a funny grin. "He said he always wanted to see the birthplace of democracy."

"Greece, huh?" He turned as the mahogany doors were unlocked and dragged open. A bald-headed man with a mouthful of gold teeth glowered at him, and Matt showed his badge. The glower didn't go away, but the man stepped back, and Matt and Jonesy stepped inside. A beefy arm barred Tara's passage.

"I'm with them," she protested.

The doorman said, "Pull the other one, sister. You're no cop. Your legs aren't bad enough."

"Nice try, Torchy Blane," Matt said. The heavy doors closed on Tara's protests.

The bruiser led them through a lounge, which opened onto an inside garden with a small waterfall, and then through to another larger lounge with a stage, where a platinum-haired girl was running through some swing versions of Christmas standards while a man at the piano tinkled along.

A man and woman sat amidst the sea of empty tables. They had the easy rapport of an old married couple, but in fact Sid Szabo and Nora Noonan were longtime business partners. The rumor was that they were lovers as well, but observing them together, Matt wasn't sure.

Nora Noonan was not beautiful, but she had a self-contained, intelligent face—like a portrait of the Madonna. Her hair was reddish blond. She wore a well-cut tweed suit. Sid Szabo was one of the handsomest men Matt had ever seen—like a Sunday matinee idol. Dark hair and eyes so blue you could tell it from across the room. He was watching the girl on the stage, but Matt knew he hadn't missed their entrance.

Nora Noonan was smiling her slight, enigmatic smile as Matt and Jonesy approached the table. "Well, Detectives, we heard the news on the radio. I had a feeling you'd be showing up."

"Lieutenant Spain," Matt said, and flashed the tin.

Nora Noonan raised her eyebrows, pretending to be impressed. "May I offer you a drink, Lieutenant Spain?"

"No thanks. What can you tell me about the Arlen kid?"

"Do sit down!" She smiled at Jonesy. "Sergeant? You look like a drinking man."

Jonesy made some uncomfortable assurances to the contrary, and she smiled that smile again. Szabo watched them, unspeaking, his eyes not missing a move—and yet his attention remained with the girl now warbling "I'll Be Home for Christmas."

After they were seated, Nora said, "The truth? I wouldn't shed any tears over Phil Arlen—except for the fact that he owed me forty grand."

Matt whistled. "Is that right? Forty thousand dollars in gambling debts?"

"Gambling is illegal in this state, Lieutenant," Nora said mildly. "This was a personal loan."

"For?"

Nora smiled. "I didn't like to ask. After all, Arlen was a good customer—and he came from a good family. I felt sure he'd make good on his debt."

"He was a weasel," Szabo said.

Nora looked exasperated. "Sid—"

"He was a weasel," Sid repeated. "Why pretend anything else?" His stone-cold eyes studied Matt boldly. "You talk to the wife? She was here Friday night threatening to kill him."

"Sid!" Nora sounded truly put out now.

Szabo turned his profile and stared at the stage and the singer. "Talk to the wife," he said.

"*Cherchez la femme,*" Nora remarked. "Maybe." She shrugged her tweed-clad shoulders. "I guess it makes as much sense as anything these days."

"The fact is, we're investigating Arlen's death as a kidnapping gone wrong," Matt said—and now he had the attention of both.

"A...kidnapping? The radio didn't mention that," Nora said carefully. Sid said nothing.

"That's right. Arlen didn't come home Saturday night. His family received a ransom demand on Sunday. The money was delivered, but Arlen was bumped off anyway."

"My goodness," Nora said faintly. "They paid the ransom?"

"Right."

Nora looked at Sid. Sid looked at Nora.

Nora said finally, "That doesn't make much sense. Killing the victim, I mean, if the ransom was paid on time. Not a sound business practice."

"That's what I say," Matt said. "Anyway, the last time anyone saw the Arlen kid was here on Saturday night."

"I wouldn't know," Nora said. "I wasn't here. I had one of my sick headaches."

She looked at Sid, who said flatly, "He was here. He was always here. We should have charged him rent."

Nora made a pained face—the Madonna putting up with a lousy suggestion from Joseph—and said, "Philip was somewhat enamored of Pearl." She nodded to the girl on the stage. "Pearl Jarvis. She sings here Tuesdays through Thursdays."

On Mondays the club was closed, and on weekends the big names appeared. The Las Palmas Club attracted a lot of big names: Tommy Dorsey, Crosby, Glenn Miller, Benny Goodman. It was one of the city's hot spots, though Matt would have to take the word of others for that. He was not much for nightclubs.

It was Szabo's turn to look irritated. "Pearl put up with the puppy, that's all. She was just being nice to a customer. They're all good girls here."

"Sure," Matt said. "Convent-reared, every one of them. So Philip hung around Pearl, and Philip's wife was jealous?"

Nora laughed a cool little laugh. "Well, I expect she wasn't *pleased* about it, but I don't think Claire Arlen is the type to go around murdering husbands."

"You might be surprised what wives will do," Matt said, holding her gaze.

Nora's dark gaze sharpened. She looked down at her drink. "True," she murmured.

Matt said to Sid, "Do you remember what time Arlen left here on Saturday?"

"I wasn't keeping track of him. He was pretty drunk, that much I do remember."

"When was the last time you remember seeing him?"

"Sometime after midnight."

"Who was he with? Pearl?" Matt glanced at the canary. She looked like a million other girls to him. Nice figure, nice face—nice voice too—but clothes too tight, hair too blond and skin too painted.

Sid smiled sourly. "Nope. They weren't talking that night. He was with a reporter. What's his name from the *Tribune-Herald.* Doyle, that's it. He was with Doyle the last time I saw him."

CHAPTER TWO

CARL WINTERS BOOKSELLER read the black-and-gold script on the sign above the long bow window. And beneath, in smaller letters: The Fine, the Rare, the Antiquarian.

Bombastic, in Nathan's opinion. The man sold words, he didn't write them. Or at least not that Nathan knew of. But then he didn't know a lot about Carl Winters. What he did know wasn't heartwarming.

He pushed through the door and found himself in one of those hushed and rarefied establishments where tomes were sold by the size and matched leather bindings—and cracking a book's spine was a hanging offense. Plush maroon carpet deadened his footsteps as he made his way through Ming vases, Chippendale chairs and a few strategically placed bookshelves to the front desk. This long black wood construction could never be called a *counter,* and nothing so plebian as a cash register sat there. A cool and elegant blonde wearing a pair of horn-rim spectacles that had to be for show observed his approach.

"May I help you?"

"I'd like to speak to Mr. Winters."

She didn't quite allow herself a smirk, but her "Did you have an appointment?" was clearly rhetorical.

"No. I'm Nathan Doyle." He showed her his press pass.

Her pointy little nose twitched. "Mr. Winters is not speaking to the press."

There was an answer to that, but Nathan bit the inside of his cheek. She didn't look like she had much sense of humor. "Okay. Well, could you remind him we met Saturday night at the Las Palmas Club?"

She tipped her head, studying him over the top of her glasses, then, reluctantly, she abandoned her front desk post and sashayed through a pair of oversized carved doors, vanishing into a discreet back room.

Nathan leaned back against the front desk and studied the very nice watercolors on the wall. England probably. A very different England than the last time he'd been there. He supposed you could still find places like that, rural pockets mostly untouched by the war. He hadn't seen any. Not in England. Not in North Africa.

Outside the shop windows, holiday shoppers in raincoats, umbrellas tilted against the rain, bustled along the wet street, laden with parcels and shopping bags. Funny, that. Come wind or rain or sleet or world wars, people still celebrated the holidays. Maybe it said something about the human spirit. Or maybe it said something about the strength of habit.

"Mr. Doyle?"

He turned as Carl Winters approached. He was alone. There was no sign of the Dresden-figurine salesgirl. That alone assured Nathan he was on the right track.

Winters was a trim and dapper midforties. He wore a pale yellow carnation in his lapel and Nathan could just about see his reflection in the gleam off Winters' hand-stained antique copper brogues. His lustrous hair was prematurely white, but the face beneath was tanned and youthful. Though he was smiling, his eyes were wary, and Nathan understood why.

They shook hands briefly, and Winters said—heading Nathan off, it seemed—"Is this a sympathy call or a request for an interview?"

Nathan studied his face. "I can't say I'm particularly sorry about Phil," he said. "Are you supposed to be?"

"He was a lowlife. A creep. That's off the record *and* on."

Nathan smiled.

"But I didn't kill him," Winters added.

"Sure. Any ideas about who might have?"

"Anyone who had the displeasure of his acquaintance."

"Including your sister?"

"Leave Claire out of this."

"She brought herself into it by showing up at the Las Palmas Club on Saturday night."

"That was…nothing," Winters said curtly.

"It was *something*." Nathan was gentle but definite. "The police are liable to think so, anyway."

Winters' face changed, grew ugly. "I see. This is a—a shakedown, is that it?"

Nathan shook his head. "I couldn't keep it quiet if I wanted to. Too many people saw your sister threaten Phil. Too many people saw all three of us at the club on Saturday."

"That's right," Winters said. "But Phil was still alive and kicking when Claire and I pulled out. We left him to *your* tender mercies."

Nathan shrugged. "Phil was alive when I left him." He considered Winters levelly. "The story is he was grabbed by kidnappers. But I guess you would have heard that from your sister."

Winters didn't so much as blink.

Nathan nodded thoughtfully. "You don't buy the kid-napping story either."

"I buy it. I'm just waiting for you to accuse me of kid-napping and murder."

"Times are tough," Nathan said. "Not many people have leisure or luxury to read these days." He glanced at a copy of William Blake's *Songs of Innocence* under glass on the ebony counter. "Not at these prices."

"I do very well," Winters said. "It's not a crime. Even in wartime."

Nathan just studied him, and Winters said edgily, "I don't know what you think you've heard…"

"We both know what Arlen was," Nathan said coolly. "I heard enough on Saturday to figure out that he was put-ting the screws on you. I can make an educated case as to what he had on you."

"What he *thought* he had on me," Winters corrected.

"If you were paying him to keep his mouth shut—and apparently you were—"

"That doesn't mean anything. I paid him because scandal can ruin a man in my position. It doesn't matter if it's true or not, just the hint of it's all it takes. That's the way the world turns."

"Maybe so." Nathan was thinking that if Winters had nothing to fear he would have told his brother-in-law to go to hell. He hadn't because he didn't want Arlen planting that seed of doubt in anyone's minds. It was liable to start people looking, and Winters couldn't afford that. Nathan understood that line of reasoning because he couldn't af-ford people to start looking either. He added, "I guess you weren't happy about the way he was treating your little sis-ter."

"No, I wasn't happy," Winters said. "But, believe it or not, Claire loved that little rat. She wouldn't have thanked me for removing him from this mortal coil." He swallowed hard. "This is liable to kill her."

"She seemed healthy enough to me on Saturday," Nathan replied. "Healthy pair of lungs on her."

Winters' face darkened again. "She didn't kill him. And I didn't kill him. And as far as paying Phil hush money, what were *you* paying him for?"

Nathan's smile was wry. "I didn't pay him. I couldn't afford to."

Winters stared at him. "Then it seems to me," he said, "you've got as good a motive for murder as anyone."

"It does seem that way," Nathan agreed.

Philip and Claire Arlen lived up the road a bit from the Robert Arlens, in a fashionable five-story Spanish-Italian apartment hotel called the Los Altos. The hand-tinted postcards sold in the lobby said the Los Altos "Catered to a Particular Clientele," which always amused the hell out of Nathan.

He ran through the stone courtyard, fountains gurgling with rain and water, and ducked under the ornate stone entrance. The lobby was carpeted in red, the walls creamy, and the light muted. A large flocked Christmas tree stood at one end, a spill of gaily wrapped, for-display-only "presents" beneath its feathery limbs. Nathan went up a couple of flights of stairs, down a hall with intricately carved wooden panels, and rang the buzzer of Philip Arlen's apartment. Veronica Thompson-Arlen opened the door.

"Oh," she said, surprised. She did not seem like a woman frequently caught off guard. She had been a navy nurse, Nathan remembered, Bob's nurse after he cracked up his B-25 Mitchell during a failed bombing run over Japan. Love among the bedpans. Bob hadn't come out of it too badly. A game leg, a scarred face, a beautiful young wife and a nice cushy job waiting for him. A lot of guys had it a lot worse.

It made sense that Veronica would be there to comfort her sister-in-law. Nathan said, "Hi, Ronnie. Is Claire home?"

"She's resting. Why?" She glanced over her shoulder into the silent interior of the apartment. The drapes were drawn, blinds closed. "Nathan, she's not well enough to speak to anyone. Phil's death has devastated her."

"I'll be careful with her."

"But why can't it wait?"

Good question. He said, "You'll have to take my word that it can't."

Veronica studied him. "I don't know you that well." Then she shrugged. "Bob says you're a straight shooter. I'll ask Claire if she feels up to talking to you." She hesitated as though there were something more she needed to say then seemed to change her mind. She turned and walked into the other room.

Nathan looked around himself. The word was that old man Arlen had cut the purse strings to young Philip in an effort to bring him into line. The way Nathan heard it, the old man wanted Philip to enter the family business— take his birthright corner office at Arlen Petroleum—and to spend a few more nights at home. It was no secret that Phil had declined. But it didn't look like he and the missus were suffering unduly. The apartment was very nice—they were all very nice apartments at the Los Altos—although it didn't come with the finger bowls and champagne glasses doled out to occupants of the Bryson. Still, it didn't look like baby brother was exactly strapped for cash. Claire's bloodline was impeccable, but the Winterses had been at financial low tide for decades, ever since the big crash in '29, so the funding wasn't coming from her side of the family.

Veronica appeared in the doorway and beckoned Nathan in.

The living room was dark; it smelled of pine trees and Elizabeth Arden. A five-foot evergreen stood unadorned in one corner, and various scattered ornaments winked and glinted in the dim light. He could just make out the woman sitting on the sofa near the French doors. Claire Arlen's hair appeared to be the exact shade of the pale carnation her brother wore in his lapel. She was fair and small and built. She wore some kind of frothy negligee set, and she looked as fragile as the Christmas tree angel sitting on the table beside her elbow.

Nathan glanced around and Veronica had disappeared.

Claire said in a dull voice, "Carl called to tell me you'd probably turn up. I didn't kill Phil."

Nathan took off his hat and sat down on the ottoman. "You were pretty upset with him on Saturday night."

"Not with Phil. With *her.* That woman."

"Pearl Jarvis?"

Claire nodded. "The torcher. 'I'm Getting Sentimental Over You.'" She laughed a bitter little laugh and covered her eyes with her hand. "I used to like that song!"

"Was Phil having an affair with her?"

"I don't know." She wiped her eyes. "I didn't think so, but then…" She shook her head. "There was something between them."

"It seemed like you thought so on Saturday night."

She took her hand down and glared at him.

He made sure his voice stayed low and soothing. "Did you ever try to talk to Pearl?"

"*Her?*" She sounded indignant. "That tramp?"

He smiled apologetically. "I know wives sometimes do—try to talk to other women."

Something in his smile seemed to disarm her instinctive affront. "Are you married?" she asked.

"No."

"Got a sweetheart?"

He shook his head. "I've been overseas."

Claire shook her head like he couldn't possibly understand. "I did try to talk to her once. She just laughed at me. Told me Phil was free, white and twenty-one. When Phil found out I'd been to see her, he slapped me. Carl told him if he ever laid a hand on me again—" She broke off.

"He'd kill him?" Nathan finished.

She didn't reply.

"I guess I'd feel the same," Nathan said. "If someone treated my sister that way."

"Do you have a sister?"

"No."

"Then what do you know about it?" She turned a mutinous profile and stared unseeingly at the row of photos on the credenza. "Anyway, it was only the one time. Carl didn't kill Phil. He was killed by the kidnappers."

"Why do you think they did that? After the ransom was paid?"

"How should I know? Maybe...Phil saw one of them. Maybe he saw or heard something and they couldn't afford to let him go. Maybe...there was a problem with the money. Maybe they didn't receive the ransom payment."

"Do you think there *was* a ransom payment?"

That brought her face forward in a hurry. "What are you suggesting?"

"Yes, what *are* you suggesting?"

That was Veronica, standing in the doorway behind him. He hadn't heard her, and he wondered how long she had been standing there.

He said simply, "Nothing the police won't think of on their own."

"Listen," Veronica said. "Regardless of what Bob thought of Phil and the way Phil conducted his affairs—sorry, Claire, honey—he wouldn't do anything to jeopardize his safety. That's not brotherly love, it's the kind of man Bob is—and you ought to know it. Bob delivered that money exactly per the kidnapper's instructions."

"I believe you," Nathan said.

"I don't care if you believe me or not. You've outstayed your welcome, Mr. Doyle."

Nathan glanced at Claire, but she seemed to have tuned out again. She was staring at the grouping of photos, her hand resting lightly on her midriff as though she felt ill—and he couldn't blame her for that. He rose and followed Veronica into the outer hallway with the Italian carvings. He put his hat on, and she said abruptly, "You're getting the wrong idea about Phil. Mostly he was just young. If Benedict had let him enlist like he wanted to, he'd have been all right. The irony is Benedict wanted to keep him safe at home."

"Just boyish high spirits, is that the story?" Nathan inquired.

She met his gaze levelly. "We all have our stories, Mr. Doyle. Don't we?"

Nathan had lunch—a drink and a smoke—at the High Hat, where most of the reporters from the larger papers hung out. It was a nice little place with decent food and strong drinks. There was a piano bar in the evenings, and out back was a red-carpeted patio with several tables beneath green umbrellas. Because of the rain, everyone was inside and the bar was noisy and blue with smoke. Most of the noise centered on the Arlen story, and Nathan took a fair amount of razzing about being picked up by the police.

He grinned, easily deflected the questions and listened closely. Everyone seemed to be running with the same angle: a kidnapping gone wrong. He hoped that meant the police were investigating it the same way. He wasn't convinced though. Lieutenant Spain seemed the thorough kind.

For a moment he let himself dwell on the thought of Lieutenant Spain. Alert, aggressive—probably an ex-marine. They were all tough bastards. But Spain had that boy-next-door quality too. And that infrequent and devastating smile—and eyes just the color of a Scottish loch at sunset, sort of green-gold, like summer bracken or polished cairngorm.

And the fact that Nathan was thinking like this about *a cop* indicated just how bad things had gotten. Maybe he really was losing his mind.

It was after two o'clock by the time Nathan caught the Yellow Car for Wilshire Boulevard and the Las Palmas Club. By then he was feeling the cumulative effect of too many drinks and too many sleepless nights. He was still a long way from being fit—there were days when he wondered if he would ever feel truly fit again. And the worst part was he didn't really care either way.

Like all such places, the Las Palmas Club seemed smaller in the daylight. Rain sheeted off its striped awning and gargled down the gutters of Wilshire.

He expected to have trouble getting into the club but, in fact, he had very little. An ugly, bald-headed bruiser let him inside and, after a brief wait in the foyer, he was shown into a leather-lined office. As he entered the room, Nora Noonan and Sid Szabo broke off what appeared to be an intense discussion. Sid swung away and went to glare out the rain-streaked window.

Nora rose from a Queen Anne chair behind an equally magnificent desk. "Mr. Doyle, you're becoming a regular."

Nathan smiled and shook hands. "I'm afraid I'm here in my official capacity."

"And what's that? Snoop?" That came from Sid, his back to the room.

"The Arlens are news in this town," Nathan said mildly.

"Of course they are." Nora shot Sid's back an exasperated look and then smiled again at Nathan. "We always like to cooperate with the press, but I'm not sure how much help we'll be. Frankly, it's not the best publicity for us, Phil Arlen getting kidnapped off our doorstep."

"Was he kidnapped?"

"The police seem to think so."

"What do you think?"

She directed another one of those looks at Sid's unresponsive broad shoulders, waiting in vain, it seemed, for him to chime in. "It seems likely. The last time anyone seems to have seen him was here."

"With you," Sid said.

Nathan turned his way. "That's right. Phil and I walked out together. We said good night. He went his way and I went mine."

"So you say."

"Sid!" That time Nora couldn't contain her impatience. The smile she turned on Nathan was apologetic and charming. "There's no reason we can't be civilized. Would you like a drink, Mr. Doyle?"

Nathan thought about it. He couldn't remember if he had eaten at all that morning. He suspected breakfast had consisted of a nip from the flask belonging to Fred Williams of the *Daily News.* And there had been several drinks after that, but the alcohol was helping him get through this—and there was still a long way to go—so he said, "Sure."

Nora poured him a generous two fingers from a bottle of Four Roses. "Sid?" she inquired.

"You know I don't drink during the day," Sid returned.

Nora winked at Nathan and took a dainty sip. She reminded Nathan of a nun with the high white collar of her blouse and her plain, intelligent face—although he'd never seen a nun taking a nip.

He said, directing the question to either of them, "What can you tell me about the relationship between Pearl Jarvis and Phil Arlen?"

"Why are you trying to start something? There was no relationship," Sid said, turning to face the room—to face Nathan. "The little weasel had a crush on Pearl. Lots of guys do."

"Mrs. Arlen seemed to think it was a little more than that."

Nora sighed. "Perhaps it was. What can it matter now? Arlen's dead."

"Yeah," Nathan said. "Supposedly his kidnappers bumped him off after they picked up the ransom money. Any idea why that would be?"

"Maybe he got on their nerves," Szabo said. "It's been known to happen."

"Maybe," Nathan agreed. "How much was Arlen into you for?"

"Forty big ones," Szabo said. "So if you're thinking Nora and I have a new sideline—"

"If you have, you came out sixty grand ahead on the deal."

Nora laughed. "We're gamblers. We're not crazy."

"I agree," Nathan said. "For that kind of risk it would have to be worth a lot more to you than sixty—or even a hundred grand." When neither of them responded, he asked, "Would it be okay if I talked to Pearl?"

"Why?" Szabo asked.

As though he hadn't spoken, Nora said, "That's up to Pearl. She's not here right now. You can probably catch her after her show this evening."

"Do you have an address for her?"

"No," Szabo said.

Nora looked regretful. "We don't give that kind of information out, Mr. Doyle. But come back this evening. We'll see you get the best seat in the house. Nothing's too good for the gentlemen of the press." She smiled a secret sort of smile.

Nathan looked at Szabo. "Any reason you don't want me to talk to Pearl?"

"Why should there be?"

Nathan shrugged. "Every time her name comes up you get a little testy. You have a lot of problems with her?"

"We don't have any problems with her."

"She's very good," Nora said. "Very talented. Have you ever heard her sing 'I'm Getting Sentimental Over You'?"

"Once or twice. She knows how to sell a song." Nathan said to Szabo, "Maybe you did like her. Maybe you liked her too much."

Szabo stared long and unblinkingly at Nathan.

Nora said, "I guess you haven't heard the rumors about Sid and me, Mr. Doyle."

Nathan smiled. "I guess I might have—but I don't believe everything I hear."

He was not going to be very popular with Whitey Whitlock, his editor. At the rate he was going, the *Tribune-Herald* was going to be the only paper in town that didn't have a major story filed on the Arlen murder. That in itself was liable to look suspicious.

He couldn't help it. He didn't have a lot of time. Every time he thought of a particular police lieutenant with a pair of shrewd hazel eyes, Nathan could hear a clock ticking. It wasn't going to take Lieutenant Spain long to put two and two together because—unless Nathan was very wrong—Lieutenant Spain already had an inkling or two.

Of course he could be letting his imagination—and guilty conscience—run away with him. He thought back to what he'd read in Spain's eyes. The look he'd first seen across the sand and weeds and grass that morning—a very different look from the one he'd seen by the time they parted ways after leaving Bob Arlen's apartment. Had he interpreted that look correctly? Or was he seeing what he wanted to see? It was hard to know sometimes.

Either way it was moot now. Spain had picked up the scent, and Nathan recognized, without knowing almost anything about the man, that Spain was a very good tracker.

There was still a chance, if he acted quickly, and that's what he had spent the morning doing.

He needed to find Pearl Jarvis. Needed to hear her story, find out what she had to say, but if she wasn't deliberately lying low, she was sure giving a good impression of it.

Having struck out at the club, he wasted another hour hunting down her last known address. But Pearl no longer resided at the rooming house in Echo Park, and Nathan got an earful from her former roommate about owed rents and a missing Bonwit Teller evening coat.

From Echo Park he trailed the elusive Miss Jarvis back to an apartment on Highland Avenue, but it was the same story—or at least a similar one—there. Miss Jarvis had vacated owing a month's rent and claiming loudly that she knew nothing about a misplaced cultured pearl choker.

Pearl was clearly a girl who moved around a lot even in Los Angeles's wartime housing shortage. But maybe she had good reason. It seemed that way to Nathan. From Highland Avenue he finally tracked her down at a rooming house on Hill Street.

But although Pearl technically still lived at Mrs. Malloy's, she was not at home.

"When do you expect her back?" he asked.

Mrs. Malloy was vague. "Not 'til after the last show to night." Her face took on a suspicious look. "No gentlemen visitors after seven o'clock."

"I wouldn't dream of it," Nathan said, and that was true.

It looked like he was going to have to settle for talking to Pearl after the last show at the Las Palmas Club.

He caught a streetcar back to Broadway and Third, pushing through the arched entrance of the Tribune-Herald Building, making his way through the inside courtyard, looking up to see rain washing across the skylight. Taking the caged elevators up, he mentally hammered out his story. He didn't have anything. He was trusting that no one else did either, but he didn't know. He hadn't noticed any extras showing up on the street, but he'd been so preoccupied, somebody could have pushed a paper into his hand and he wouldn't have noticed.

Had the cops managed to talk to Pearl? Something Szabo had said before Nathan left the Las Palmas Club made him think not. Not then, anyway. But even if the cops talked to Pearl, they might not know which questions to ask. In fact, Nathan was trusting that they didn't, that they were still investigating Arlen's murder as a kidnapping gone wrong.

Whitey Whitlock greeted him with the usual inquiry as to whether he could explain why they were paying him such an exorbitant salary to sit on his duff and drink martinis at the High Hat all day.

Doyle assured Whitlock he had no idea, but he personally felt he was worth every penny. Then he sat down and typed up some malarkey, handed it in to Whitlock, who scowled from beneath white and beetling brows as he skimmed the crisply typed pages and shook his head.

"Doesn't anyone in this town know *anything*?"

"If they do, they're not talking to the press."

Whitlock didn't say the obvious, that it had taken Nathan all goddamned day to file a story any cub reporter could have turned in his first day on the job. In the old days Nathan would have had his ass canned for that kind of omission, but with the manpower shortage, and the war effort dominating every front page, he had a little room to operate. And, while he wouldn't have previously thought to trade on it, his bloodstained resume gave him a certain amount of clout at the *Tribune-Herald*.

He told Whitlock that since every paper in town was covering the story, he was hoping to get the human-interest angle. Whitlock looked skeptical, and rightly so. Nathan hadn't given any previous indication of anything so unwholesome as an interest in humans, but he contented himself with shaking his head and muttering how he'd always known it was a mistake to hire Doyle.

And then, very off-handedly, he mentioned that the police had been there looking for him—twice.

Nathan stood still. Then he realized that Whitlock was watching him, and he raised his brows. "I can't uncover *all* their leads for them," he said.

Whitlock harrumphed. "Next time meet them at your other office. They bring down the tone of the place." He retreated, muttering, to his lair, and Nathan went to the men's room and splashed cold water on his face.

He needed to eat something. That was the first priority. And then he needed to see what the cops wanted. But, of course, he knew what they wanted. They wanted to know why he hadn't mentioned he was one of the last people to see Phil Arlen alive. They would have found that out right after they visited the Las Palmas Club.

There had never been any question he was going to have to have this conversation with Lieutenant Spain, but it was better to go into it prepared, so he drank some water and headed downstairs to the newspaper morgue where he looked up everything he could find on Lt. Mathew Spain.

There wasn't a lot. He learned that Spain was thirty-five—a few years older than himself—and had been a cop for ten years before he enlisted in the marines, had been hit by sniper fire on Guadalcanal, and he returned to the Los Angeles police force, who were, apparently, so delighted to have him back they'd promoted him to lieutenant.

Mathew. Matt.

It suited him. Nathan stared down at the black-and-white photo. It was a tough face, but an intelligent one. Keen eyes—you could see it even in black and white. A stubborn chin, a full—but grim—mouth. Not a guy who gave up easily—if at all. It was a mouth that looked like it had learned the hard way not to smile too easily. It was an attractive face and it was hard to remember that this was the face of an adversary.

The hungry, restless feeling was on him again. For a few months in hospital he'd hoped—prayed—he was cured, but it was worse since he'd returned to Los Angeles. Much worse. Need was like a fever burning him up, burning up his inhibitions, his common sense, his instinct for self-preservation. Ironically, the war had kept him reasonably sane, reasonably steady. But now he was back to where he'd started.

He needed to give Lt. Mathew Spain a call.

But first he decided to go down to the Biltmore for a couple of drinks.

Chapter Three

"**W**hat have you got for me on the Arlen kid?"

Doc Mason shoved a file cabinet closed and locked it. "Straightforward, as far as it goes. There's a bruise on his jaw like someone socked him, but that's the only sign of a struggle. He was shot from the front, from about six feet away. Hands were down at his side when he was hit. That might be significant or not. I leave it to you boys to decide. The bullet lodged in the heart. Didn't exit the body. Here's the interesting part." The coroner moved to the long counter and waved a long pair of tweezers holding a misshapen slug of lead in front of Matt's nose.

Matt's eyes narrowed. "What the hell's that?"

Mason smiled. "That, Lieutenant, is a .17, 4.3 mm ball."

"A homemade bullet?"

"Possibly. But I think it's the real McCoy."

Matt said slowly, "You think the Arlen kid was shot with an antique pistol?"

"I'm guessing a derringer."

Matt thought it over. A reluctant smile tugged at his mouth. "Swell."

"I knew you'd appreciate it."

"When was he killed?"

"Ah." Mason dropped the bullet into a small card-board container. "Monday evening. I'd say after midnight."

"After the ransom was delivered."

"That's the way it adds up."

"Or doesn't," Matt said.

"They haven't seen Doyle at the *Tribune-Herald* since this morning," Jonesy informed Matt when he entered Matt's office later that afternoon. "He showed up long enough to turn in a story about the Arlen kid floating in the Brea Pit, and they haven't seen him since. I get the impression he comes and goes as he pleases."

Matt raised his eyebrows. "Must be nice."

"They like him over there," Jonesy admitted. "I gave them plenty of opportunity to say otherwise."

"What do you think of Sid Szabo?"

"I've heard things, but nobody ever suggested he ran a crooked joint. That counts for something in this town."

"How reliable a witness do you think Nora Noonan is?"

"On the stand or from my perspective?"

"From your perspective."

Jonesy studied him. "I think Arlen left the Las Palmas Club with Doyle on Saturday night."

"Yeah." Matt sighed. "He lied by omission. I can't think of a good reason for him not to mention he was with the Arlen kid on Saturday night."

"What do you think he was doing out at the Arlen estate this morning?"

Matt had been wondering about that himself. People got skittish in murder investigations—and not always for the obvious reasons. But Doyle didn't strike him as the skittish type. The opposite, in fact, which he thought was proved by Doyle's visit to the Arlen estate.

"That's what I plan on asking him the first chance I get." He smiled at Jonesy's suspicious expression. "What do you know about Nora Noonan?"

"She came to L.A. in '37. Partnered up with Szabo. They started the Las Palmas Club together and it was a hit from the night it opened."

"She's from Denver originally," Matt said. "Used to sing in the supper clubs. She was married to a cardsharp by the name of Stephen Reilly. The story is Reilly used to get drunk and slap Noreen—as she was called then—around, and one night she had enough of it and used a Remington Springfield on him. Claimed she thought he was a burglar. There was a trial, but Noreen was a popular lady, and she was acquitted due to insufficient evidence. She changed her first name to Nora, went back to using her maiden name and came out west where she hooked up with Szabo."

"Cripes," Jonesy said. "The things you pick up. You ever think of joining the police force?"

"Ha."

"Can't see she had much reason for getting rid of Arlen, Loot. Especially when he owed forty thousand in gambling debts."

"Yeah, but did you get a look at how old those notes were?"

Jonesy shook his head.

"A couple of them were nearly a year old. Why did Szabo and Noonan keep extending him credit when he wasn't paying up?"

"I don't see how he could have paid up," Jonesy said. "From what I can make out, he never worked a day in that big office his father gave him at Arlen Petroleum. And according to the brother, the old man had cut the kid off to try and put some backbone into him."

"There was money from his mother, but he went through that in the first year after she passed away."

Silence.

"You want me to bring Doyle in?" Jonesy said.

Matt thought it over. "He can wait. I think I'm ready to talk to the wife now. It sounds to me like, at the least, she took a dim view of his gambling. And see if you can locate the singer, Pearl Jarvis. I didn't like the way she happened to slip out the back door while we were interviewing Noonan and Szabo. If she and Arlen really weren't on speaking terms that night, I want to know why. Either way, I want to know what was between them."

"That dame must have something going for her," Jonesy said. "I get the feeling Szabo's sweet on her too."

"To each his own," Matt said, and thought of Nathan Doyle.

"**I** found some letters from her once," Claire Arlen was saying dully. "Awful things. Violet paper, purple ink… doused in scent." She shivered—although that could have been due to the skimpy silk dressing gown she wore. The apartment was cold, and the only light was the one Claire Arlen had turned on when Spain and Jonesy had turned up at her door.

Someone should have been staying with her, in Matt's opinion. But maybe she didn't want anyone. He hadn't wanted anyone after Rachel.

"And these letters were to your husband?"

She looked surprised, as though the other possibility had never occurred to her. "I thought so at the time. Phil said no. I didn't believe him…but now I wonder." Large green eyes—so pale a green that they looked gray—turned Matt's way. "There was no name, you see. They were just addressed 'darling.'"

"Why would your husband have these letters if they weren't his?"

Claire shook her head. "I don't know. But Phil said they weren't his."

Matt nodded. He was beginning to form a certain ugly idea about Phil Arlen. It had to do with gambling debts no one tried to collect on, and love letters that might not have been his.

Claire said, "I know what everyone thinks, that Phil wouldn't have married me if his father hadn't insisted, but it's not true. We were happy together. Mostly."

"What happened when you went to the Las Palmas Club on Saturday night?"

She stared at him like she didn't understand the question.

"You went to the club and had words with Phil."

"I had words with *her*," Claire said. "I told her that if she didn't stop—"

"If she didn't stop," Matt prompted.

"I...would go to Phil's dad." Her expression was a little defiant. "Mr. Arlen is a very powerful man. He could arrange things so that little floozy would never work again."

Was floozy the kind of job that required good references? Matt doubted it, but he refrained from saying so. "You didn't threaten to kill her or Phil?"

"I might have." She waved that away almost absently. "I got a little hysterical when Carl tried to drag me out before I'd finished. But it was just...talk. I'd had two cocktails with supper, and I've never had a head for strong spirits." She pressed her hands to her temple as though the very thought of strong spirits was making her head spin.

"Do you own a gun, Mrs. Arlen?"

"Of course not!"

"Did your husband own a gun?"

"No."

"Your father-in-law told us that a woman called to say your husband had been kidnapped. Did you recognize the voice? Any idea as to who that woman might have been?"

Claire shook her head dully.

"If your husband and Miss Jarvis weren't lovers, what do you think their relationship was?"

Again Claire shook her head.

"Do you have any idea why the kidnappers would have killed your husband after the ransom was paid?"

"No."

"Do you have any reason to think the ransom might not have been paid?"

She looked up, wide-eyed. "That's just what that reporter suggested."

Matt and Jonesy exchanged looks. "Doyle?" Matt asked. "From the *Tribune-Herald?*"

"That's right. He's a friend of Bob's. Or he was. He was at the club that night too. I suppose he thought I was too upset to remember, but I remember. He was there, and he was plenty mad himself. I know." She met Matt's gaze steadily. "He was smiling, but he was bone white—and his eyes were…glittering." She gave a little shiver. "I don't know *why,* but I do know he was mad enough to kill."

Matt didn't say anything. Then he glanced at Jonesy. "I think maybe it's time to have another word with Mr. Doyle," he said.

Mr. Doyle had still not returned to roost at the *Tribune-Herald.* The address the paper had on file for him turned out to be his mother's Adam's Hill residence in Glendale.

The house was one of those old-fashioned English-style cottages: red brick with white-trimmed windows and doors. Tidy hedges surrounded the house, and instead of lawn there was neatly trimmed ivy. Christmas lights were draped along the shingled roof of the house.

Mrs. Doyle was tall and thin and fair. She had the elegant bone structure and same light, restless gaze as her son. She took policemen on her welcome mat with remarkable cool, inviting them into an immaculate living room. Matt looked around. Plastic covers on all the lamp shades and antimacassars on the arms of the chairs and sofa. Three pictures of Nathan Doyle at various ages hung in a corner over a large white statue of the Blessed Virgin. Eleven pictures of Jesus at various ages took up the rest of the wall space. A large nativity sat on a long table behind the sofa.

Nathan, Mrs. Doyle informed them, had moved to his own place on Bunker Hill. She offered them tea and cookies, apparently as a consolation prize, and to Jonesy's astonishment, Matt accepted her invitation and made himself comfortable across from the photos of Nathan Doyle. Even as a kid, Doyle had been serious-looking, but then Mrs. Doyle didn't look like a lot of laughs.

Mrs. Doyle carried in a tea tray and set it down on the table. China cups and a lovely china teapot with purple pansies kept a plate of Girl Scout cookies company.

"How is your son adjusting to civilian life?" Matt asked.

Mrs. Doyle fixed him with those cool eyes so like her son's. "Nathan is a realist," she said, which he thought was sort of strange. "Were you in the service?"

Matt admitted that he had been, and she asked him a number of interested questions, and then talked to him about the care packages the church was sending to servicemen all over the world. It was not that she declined to discuss her son; she just managed to answer with as little information as possible. Matt had a fair bit of experience with interrogation, but he suspected Mrs. Doyle could probably hold her own against the SS.

Still, it was interesting seeing the home Nathan Doyle had grown up in. Matt wasn't sure if it would prove relevant, but he didn't regret listening to Mrs. Doyle talk—although he could feel Jonesy's unease. Jonesy took a dim view of Catholics and their arcane ways.

Finally, when they had eaten the last Girl Scout cookie and drunk the last of the tea, Mrs. Doyle said, "I suppose you'll want to see his room?"

She supposed right, but Matt was mildly grateful she'd taken the initiative. Then again, Mrs. Doyle didn't strike him as a lady who ducked unpleasant duty. He accepted the offer, rising, and Mrs. Doyle led them down a short hall and up a short flight of steps—the house was oddly laid out—to a room overlooking the quiet street.

As Matt would have expected, the room was spotlessly neat. A large crucifix of a particularly handsome—but tortured—Christ hung over the crisply made bed. Matt examined the bookshelves. A number of catechism books, tomes on the saints' lives rubbed shoulders with well-worn copies of the Hardy Boys, Tom Swift, and the Radio Boys novels. A large framed map of the world hung on the wall across from the bed—the first thing young Nathan would have opened his eyes to every morning growing up? There were a few class pictures in frames, and a couple of model airplanes. Matt looked around himself, but could get no feel for the boy Nathan Doyle must have been.

He had forgotten Mrs. Doyle was watching them. "He was very badly wounded, you know. They didn't think he would live." She spoke quietly from the doorway, and Matt turned. "I don't think he has quite got used to the idea himself."

"What happened?"

"I don't know. He never speaks of it. They gave him a medal. The George Medal. For civilian bravery. He won't speak of that either. I think he's a little ashamed. Newspaper men are supposed to be neutral, and in the end, he wasn't."

Matt moved toward the door.

She said, "Whatever you think he's done, you're wrong. Nathan is a good man. A man of honor."

Matt said only, "Thank you for letting me see this, ma'am."

"No wonder he went off his rocker," Jonesy remarked as they headed over to Bunker Hill.

Matt glanced at him, but didn't answer.

"From the first minute I saw him, I sort of thought something might not be right with him," Jonesy pursued. "You get an instinct for it."

"I don't see any obvious motive for him wanting the Arlen kid out of the way, but I also can't see any reason for him to have concealed the fact he was at the club. But people hide things in a homicide investigation. They get spooked. It doesn't always mean they've committed murder."

He remembered his father and Jonesy telling him this very thing many years before, but Jonesy looked unconvinced now. And Matt wasn't convinced himself.

Doyle lived in an apartment in one of the original Victorian houses on Olive Street.

Matt and Jonesy identified themselves, and the apartment manager led them upstairs into a chilly room with large bay windows overlooking what must have once been a lovely garden. In the center of the room was an unmade pull-down bed and a table with a typewriter, a half-full bottle of Teacher's blended Scotch whisky beside it.

No pictures and no religious icons. A tall bookshelf stood mostly empty except for a couple of Christmas cards, a parcel wrapped in reindeer paper, and several volumes on travel and history and archeology. The books included a copy of the dialogs of Plato and Thomas Aquinas.

You could tell a lot about a man by what he chose to read, in Matt's opinion. He liked a good Western himself, but it was a long time since he'd read any.

More books were stacked on the table, a couple of medical books, and books on psychology. A book lying next to the bed bore the title *The Homosexual Neurosis*.

"Thanks very much," Matt said to the apartment manager. "We'll take it from here." He turned, nudging the book beneath the bed with the toe of his shoe, and forced the man out into the hall, nearly closing the door on the end of his inquisitive nose.

He leaned back against the door, and realized his heart was pounding hard and heavily, as though he'd barely escaped some terrible threat.

"Couple of bottles of painkillers in the bathroom, Loot." Jonesy poked his head out. "Nothing illegal."

Matt nodded.

"Did you find something?" Jonesy asked him.

"Huh? No." He turned away from Jonesy's curious gaze and opened the drawer of a built-in dresser. A neatly wrapped Walther rested amidst some carefully folded sweaters and corduroys. A beautiful weapon. Modern and efficient. The kind of weapon he personally would choose if he was going to commit murder.

But to each his own.

He closed the drawer again. Rain dripped soothingly from the eaves above the windows. Despite the physical temperature of Doyle's quarters, this room was more alive and warm than the room he had spent his boyhood in. He could feel Doyle here—feel him too well.

"Nothing," Jonesy muttered from the bathroom, and for the first time Matt wondered if Jonesy was losing his touch. Of course, if it hadn't been for the war, Jonesy would have retired by now. But it was harder than hell to find good men these days.

Jonesy rejoined him in the main room. "I guess he didn't kill Arlen for the money," he remarked as they stared around the monklike setting. "It's like a barracks in here."

Matt nodded.

They went downstairs and spoke to the building manager once more.

"Quiet. Keeps to himself. No problems." The little man licked his lips. "Is there something I should know?"

Matt thought of the book he had shoved under the bed. He had thought of putting it under the mattress, but Doyle was liable to panic when he didn't find it. And the last thing he wanted to do was panic Doyle. Not with a gun in his drawer and a medicine chest full of painkillers.

"No," he said firmly. "This was just a routine check." Like LAPD routinely inspected for dust or something. "Please tell Mr. Doyle to get in contact with us when he has a chance."

The little man nodded doubtfully.

"When he has a *chance?*" Jonesy repeated when they went outside.

"I don't want that nosey parker going through Doyle's rooms."

Jonesy didn't answer.

Matt said, "Let's get a photograph of Pearl Jarvis and show it around."

"Okey dokey," Jonesy said slowly, still looking at him.

It was quite a while after he'd told Jonesy good night when Matt decided to head over to the Biltmore Hotel Bar.

Doyle's editor had told them that Doyle sometimes went there after work. Matt had hung around headquarters for longer than necessary on the chance Doyle might call, although he hadn't really expected Doyle would make the effort to get hold of him that evening. It was clear to him by now what secret Doyle was guarding.

And Doyle's secret confirmed what Matt already suspected of Phil Arlen.

He tried to put himself in Doyle's shoes, but he couldn't. He thought Phil Arlen was no loss to the world.

Doyle must surely know that they had gone to his workplace—he might even know that they had visited his mother and his apartment. In his position...well, it was hard to picture being in Doyle's position. Matt wasn't sure he wanted to.

The Biltmore Hotel was known as The Host of the Coast, and that night it did indeed seem to be hosting the entire population of California—or at least most of the men in the armed services.

Matt ordered a beer and found himself a quiet table in a corner. It was a beautiful room, lots of warm wood and gold leaf. There were marble floors and hand-painted ceiling frescoes and chandeliers—the kind of thing Matt would have expected to see in a museum—and there was Nathan Doyle way down at the far end of the bar, knocking back highballs with a handsome dark-haired man in a naval uniform adorned with the gold-and-silver insignia of a commander.

Doyle was clearly getting plastered. His face was flushed and his eyes were bright. He was smiling, but it was the quality of the smile that fascinated Matt. He had seen Doyle smile once or twice—always as though he had been caught off guard—but this smile was young and frank and...flirtatious.

He and the naval commander could have been alone in the packed bar; he was oblivious to Matt's presence, let alone his attention. Matt could have been standing right next to him. Instead, Matt stayed in his quiet corner, gently and not-so-gently repelling the advances of a few dames on the prowl, sipping his beer and watching. After some time and a second beer, Doyle and his friend left the bar, weeding their way through the crowd, and Matt rose and followed them out through the lobby with its parquet floors and rich jewel-toned carpets and carved ceilings, down the steps through the arches and columns into the damp night.

Doyle walked with the careful steadiness of the seasoned inebriate. The naval commander was in a little worse shape, stumbling a little and laughing, his voice bouncing back to Matt in the eerily empty street.

Matt dropped back a little. They were making for Pershing Square. Five acres of banana trees, eucalyptus and coco palms. In the daytime, the wide lawns and broad walks were busy with pedestrians, kids feeding birds, and radicals on soapboxes preaching at the top of their lungs about everything from communism to the end of the world.

But at night...at night it was another world. The walkways gleamed white in the moist moonlight, the benches sat empty, the soapboxes were vanished, and the fountain splashed in an echoing silence. And in the underbrush beneath the forest of close-growing trees and plants...

Doyle and his companion disappeared into a copse of banana trees. Matt trailed them still more slowly. He told himself he was simply doing his job, and if he was somehow discovered, he could simply arrest Doyle and his pal—although there was nothing simple about it. The idea sickened him.

But then his own actions sickened him. What the hell was he doing pushing through the stalks and waxy flowers of banana trees in pursuit of these men? He stopped, concealed in shadow and leaves, watching as Nathan dropped his trousers and got down on his hands and knees. The other man unzipped and knelt behind him, momentarily blocking Matt's view.

Matt couldn't move. The scent of decaying leaves and fruit pulp was all around him, and he felt nauseated, almost dizzy. But he had to see, so he stepped cautiously, soundlessly, keeping an eye out for other men twisting and humping in the underbrush.

Pershing Square had always been notorious for this, and now with the military in town, it was worse.

When Matt had repositioned himself, he had a perfect view of Nathan Doyle in a little circle of moonlight on his hands and knees getting fucked like a dog. He was even whimpering like a dog as the other man shoved in and out of him. Helpless, inarticulate cries—was it pleasure or pain or both?

Matt's heart seemed to thud in counterpoint, and he couldn't have looked away to save his life.

Face ricked, Doyle writhed and wriggled back on the huge cock impaling him—the other man's face was in shadow, but his powerful body was beautiful even in this obscene moment as he thrust fiercely, rhythmically into Nathan. His grunts carried through the banana leaves, and Matt wondered if he was imagining the sharp scent of sex mingled with damp earth.

And all the while Doyle kept up that puling.

It was sick and sad, and Matt knew he shouldn't be watching this, but he couldn't look away. He was miserably aware that he was getting hard—rock hard.

Doyle made another of those desperate mewling sounds. He shifted his weight and put his hand to his cock, working himself frantically, trying not to overbalance as the other man continued to slam into him.

He came first and then the other man came, collapsing on top of him, taking them both down to the ground. They lay there in the dampness, breathing hard.

Matt wiped his forehead, surprised to find that it was wet. At last the naval officer moved, rolling off Nathan and pushing up.

They didn't speak. The officer tucked himself back in, zipped up. Neither of them looked at the other as Doyle dressed hastily. The commander said something, and Doyle muttered something back, and the navy whites vanished into the trees. Doyle got up and went the other way, and Matt pulled himself together and followed.

He saw Doyle cut quickly across the cross-shaped plaza. He was making for Bunker Hill and home—making for the Angel's Flight funicular on Third and Hill, and it seemed to Matt that never had public transportation been so accurately named.

CHAPTER FOUR

The rumble of tanks and guns in the pitchy blackness, lorries and jeeps bumping along over the shifting sand—no lights allowed but the distant twinkle of the stars far overhead. Clouds of dust drifting ghostlike in the night, the forlorn yips of a jackal, the quiet murmur of voices…

Bam. Bam. Bam.

Nathan rolled out of bed, heart thundering, throat dry, groping for—

He was in a room, four walls, a ceiling, windows—he was crouching on a wooden floor next to an unmade bed. The room was soft with rosy light; the eucalyptus tree outside the window threw gentle brown shadows against the creamy walls. His books were stacked on the floor and shelves, a bottle of whisky stood on the table next to his typewriter.

He was in Los Angeles. He was home.

And someone was banging on his door.

Nathan stood, fighting to get the rush of adrenaline under control. He felt sick and shaky with it—all that fear and energy with no place to go. He sucked in a deep, steadying breath and went to the door.

"Yeah?"

A deep voice floated through the wooden barrier. "Police. Open up."

He closed his eyes, then pulled himself together and unlocked the door. Two uniformed officers stood there.

"Nathan Doyle?"

He nodded.

"You're wanted downtown for questioning."

"Am I under arrest?"

"We can do it that way if you want," the larger of the two cops said.

Nathan shook his head. "Just wondering if I have time to brush my teeth."

"We'll even give you time to pull your pants on." That was the second cop, shorter, younger, more hostile. Nathan stared at him, wondering why he wasn't in the service, wondering if the comment about his pants was intended as a crack.

"Thanks," he said coolly.

He stepped into the bathroom, bracing his hands on the sink and taking a couple of deep breaths, steadying himself.

It looked like he was out of time. He had wasted yesterday—Wednesday—dodging the cops and trying to find Pearl Jarvis. And then last night, giving in to loneliness and nerves, he had gone back to the Biltmore hoping to find the naval officer who looked so much like Lt. Mathew Spain. That had been stupid for a couple of reasons. Stupid to risk going back so soon, stupid to try for a repeat performance, and stupid most of all to acknowledge even to himself his attraction to an LAPD lieutenant. A cop. A married cop at that.

Jesus. What was next? Unrequited love?

Last night he'd found his comfort and companionship in the brawny arms of a senior airman he'd met on the steps of the hotel on his way out.

"Sam." The man had insisted they exchange names. Nathan had used his middle name, "Finan." Named for a disciple of St. Brendan. Finan was supposed to be a patron saint of monasteries, which was a good joke on someone. Sam had fucked Nathan in the banana trees of Pershing Square, and then he had tried to convince Nathan to come back to his flea-bitten hotel, and horrifyingly, Nathan had been tempted. He dreaded the idea of coming back here, of the silence and emptiness of this apartment building at night—just once he'd wanted to spend the night held tight in someone's arms, safe for a few hours, loved for a few hours—or at least pretending that he was loved.

But he'd resisted the temptation, and here he was, safe at home in time for the police to pick him up.

He could hear the cops talking quietly in his bedroom. Nathan turned on the taps, splashed cold water on his face. He shaved, brushed his teeth, ran a comb through his hair, taking no more than three minutes—he'd learned to do this fast and in the dark. His mind raced ahead to what waited for him downtown.

They hadn't tried to put handcuffs on him yet. Did that mean he wasn't being arrested? Surely that was a good sign? But the morning was young.

He dressed quickly, fingers steady, focused on what and how much of the truth he could afford to tell. He would be talking to Matt Spain. That was both the good news and the bad news.

He pushed open the door to the bathroom and the two cops broke off what they were saying to each other and eyed him warily.

The three of them went downstairs, Nathan's landlord and neighbors watching silently from their doorways. He was grateful once again that they hadn't handcuffed him, and if that was due to Matt Spain, he owed him one.

Nathan climbed into the back of the big black Ford. The young cop got behind the wheel, the older cop in back beside Nathan. Nathan listened absently as the officers talked back and forth.

"No Christmas lights at Christmas Tree Lane this year," the younger one commented as they drove down the streets decked in garlands.

The older cop said gravely, "You do know there's no Santy Claus, right, Sullivan?"

The younger cop reddened and fell silent.

Spain was alone in his office when Nathan was shown in. He nodded to Nathan's police escort, who backed out, shutting the door behind them.

"Sit down," Spain said, and Nathan took a chair across from the orderly desk. Spain looked crisp and clean-shaven in a navy suit. The wedding band on his left hand shone brightly.

"Coffee?" Spain asked politely. "Smoke?"

"Thanks."

Spain poured him a cup of coffee from a flask. Nathan sipped, and the coffee, cut with chicory, wasn't bad, though nothing as good as pre-rationing coffee. The lieutenant had a nice set-up here. Nathan's eyes were drawn to the photograph of a dark-haired woman on the bookshelf behind the desk. She looked pretty. She looked like the kind of wife someone like Lt. Mathew Spain would have. The bookshelf was full of books on the law and police procedure.

Spain proffered a pack of Camels. Nathan took one, and Spain leaned forward to light it for him. Spain's hands were large and well shaped. His lashes made dark crescents against his cheekbones. As though he felt Nathan's stare, he raised his eyes—and Nathan couldn't look away.

He stared into Mathew Spain's long-lashed hazel eyes, and he realized with terrible clarity that Spain knew all about him. Knew exactly what he was. Knew it as surely as though Nathan's ugly history were an open file on Spain's tidy desk. In fact…Nathan glanced at Spain's desktop as though somehow the explanation could be found there, because how did Spain know? *How?* Had it become that obvious? Like a scarlet letter branded into his skin—or the mark of Cain?

Hot blood flushed Nathan's face, and just as quickly drained away, leaving him feeling light-headed. He drew back, drawing sharply on his cigarette. He sat very straight.

Spain flicked his lighter closed, put it away. He seemed to be in no hurry.

"Why am I here?" Nathan blew out a stream of blue smoke. His voice was just about steady.

Spain watched him, eyes very direct beneath his straight black eyebrows. "Why didn't you mention you were with the Arlen kid on Saturday night?"

"I wasn't with him," Nathan said. "I ran into him at the Las Palmas Club. We had a drink together." He shrugged.

"Were you with him when Claire Arlen and her brother showed up?"

Nathan hesitated. "Me and half the bar."

"What happened?"

"Claire arrived with her brother, Carl, and asked Phil to come home. He declined. She got upset and said some things. She'd been drinking, I think. Anyway, Carl convinced her to leave. That's pretty much it."

Spain grinned, a white and charmingly crooked grin. All at once he looked a lot younger and a lot friendlier. "Well, that's a very careful, factual recounting of what took place. I bet you're a pretty good reporter. You understand the power of words. Other people we've interviewed have used words like 'screamed' and 'threatened' and 'demanded.'"

"Like I said, she'd had a few drinks. Her brother took her home before she could get into any real trouble."

Spain leaned back in his swivel chair and rubbed his chin. "Listen, Sir Galahad, it might interest you to know that the lady in question didn't mind throwing you to the wolves. She said it looked to her like you were pretty angry with Philip yourself. Like you were mad enough to kill."

"She doesn't know me very well." Nathan studied the ashes on his cigarette.

"Did she threaten to kill her husband and Pearl Jarvis?"

"She might have." Nathan smiled wryly. "I wasn't listening that carefully, to tell you the truth."

"Why's that?"

Nathan said slowly, "I went there for a few drinks and some laughs, but after I got there...I realized that really wasn't what I needed."

"What did you need?" Spain asked—and Nathan, for the life of him, couldn't think of how to answer.

Neither of them spoke. Neither of them looked away.

Nathan's heart was jerking like a marlin on the end of a very short line; he felt as though it was going to slip the hook and go banging around his rib cage.

The door opened behind him, and the tall gray-haired detective Spain had called Jonesy stuck his head in. "Loot, the Jarvis girl never came home last night either," he said.

"Looks like she's lying low," Spain said. "She didn't turn up for her show at the Las Palmas Club last night again."

"You think something happened to her?" Jonesy didn't sound too worried about it.

"Maybe." Spain looked at Nathan. "But according to you, Mrs. Arlen wasn't mad enough to really hurt anybody. And I can't see why anyone else needs to get rid of the late Mr. Arlen's girlfriend. Can you?"

He was baiting Nathan a little, but not offensively so.

"Maybe she knew who kidnapped Arlen." Nathan wondered whether they had already interviewed Pearl and this was merely a follow-up, or if they hadn't questioned her at all yet. He suspected they hadn't questioned her at all, because as far as he could tell, she'd already skipped town.

It occurred belatedly to him that Spain probably knew he'd been trying to find Pearl too.

"Yeah," Spain was saying thoughtfully. "Those kidnappers."

"You don't think he was kidnapped?" Nathan glanced back at Jonesy. He was leaning against the office wall, arms folded. He could feel that Jonesy didn't like him, could feel it in the way Jonesy watched him. He couldn't tell how Spain felt about him.

"I like to keep an open mind," Spain mused. He looked at Jonesy too, although he spoke to Nathan. "So tell me what happened after Mrs. Arlen made her threats and was escorted home by her brother."

"Miss Jarvis returned to her table and friends. Not long after that they all left."

"So she wasn't with Arlen?"

"They didn't speak once as far as I noticed. She doesn't perform there on the weekends, she was there as a guest like anyone else."

"How long after she left before Arlen left?"

Nathan recognized this for the trap it was.

"Maybe half an hour. Phil and I walked outside together. We said good night. He walked east. I walked west. The next time I saw him he was lying in the grass at Brea Tar Pits. Dead."

Spain glanced past Nathan to Jonesy. "Did anyone follow him? Any cars start up along the street?"

Nathan was tempted to lie, to make up a story that might keep them off his back for a while, but he shook his head. "I didn't see anything."

Silence.

Nathan smoked his cigarette, waiting, refusing to indicate by so much as a flicker of eyelash how tense he was. Unless they knew about Phil Arlen, all they had on him was the fact that he'd left the club when Arlen had. It wasn't enough to hold him, let alone charge him.

But if they had already found out how young Phil supplemented his income, then they had him. Spain already suspected what Nathan was—and he could arrest him on suspicion alone.

"Why didn't you tell us you were with the Arlen kid?" Spain asked again, and his voice was a little harsher. "It looks a little suspicious from our perspective, if you see what I mean."

"A lot of people were there that night," Nathan said. "I guess I didn't think I had anything important to tell. I knew you'd find out about it, so it's not like I was trying to hide anything."

Jonesy snorted. Nathan glanced back at him, stubbed his cigarette out, declining to respond.

"Anything else you want to tell us?" Spain asked finally.

Nathan looked up, and knew his surprised look gave the game away, but he couldn't help it. Of course he should have told them he was with Arlen. Of course his actions looked suspicious. Of course he was hiding something. He knew it. They knew it. So what was going on? Meeting Spain's eyes again, he understood that Spain wasn't fooled for one minute, but for some reason he was letting him walk away. For now.

Nathan replied, "No."

"Okay." Spain nodded politely, and Nathan rose, picking up his hat. "We'll be in touch," Spain added.

Nathan nodded and went out. The door swung gently closed behind him.

He expected to be followed, and although he could see no sign of a tail, he took it for granted that he was shadowed. It didn't present an immediate problem. Stopping for breakfast at a diner, he treated himself to eggs and bacon, not because he was hungry but because he knew he had to keep his energy up. He paid with cash and his red stamp coupons—practically the first he'd used since getting back—and then had a cup of real coffee, watching through the Christmas-painted windows as a phalanx of P-38 Lightnings headed out toward the ocean.

Despite his fatigue, he needed to get over to the paper. He felt weirdly numb, but when he thought of the night before in Pershing Square, he knew he wasn't nearly numb enough. And when he *was* that numb, the best thing would be to take that liberated Walther paratrooper Harry Ryan had given him, put it in his mouth and pull the trigger.

He rubbed his forehead tiredly, thought about Mathew Spain. Thought about the look in his eyes and the tone of his voice when he'd said, "What did you need?"

For a minute he let himself believe what he thought he'd seen, but it was too dangerous to kid himself about that.

Finishing his coffee, he left the restaurant. He would go to the paper, and he'd turn in some kind of story on the Arlen investigation, and then he'd try again to find Pearl Jarvis.

"Well, well," Jonesy said. "I think we have a winner."

Matt looked up, distracted from his own thoughts. "Is that so? What do you think Doyle's motive is?"

"It'll turn up soon enough. He's a cool customer, but it'll turn up."

They both knew motive was the least important element in putting together a case. People killed for all kinds of reasons that didn't make any sense to other people. If the means and opportunity were there, you could generally come up with a motive that would serve to convince a jury. All the same, Matt preferred his prime suspects to have strong and compelling reasons for their crimes. He preferred to believe in their guilt as he built his case.

Jonesy said, "He tried to protect Arlen's wife. Could there be something there?"

"No." Matt realized that was too final. "I doubt it." At the expression on Jonesy's face, he said, "We've got plenty of suspects. Don't make your mind up too fast."

"It's mighty convenient him walking out of the club the same time as the Arlen kid. If he wasn't the last person to see Arlen alive, he was damn close to it."

Matt said slowly, "He's not well. Not strong. I'm pretty sure Arlen wouldn't have gone with him without a fight, and I don't think Doyle could have taken him."

"According to Doc Mason the Arlen kid had a bruise on his jaw."

"That doesn't sound like much of a fight."

Jonesy conceded, "I guess if they'd actually tangled, Doyle would be carrying a few bruises. Of course, he could have taken him at gunpoint."

"True." Matt thought it over. "Or maybe the kid wasn't beat up because he went willingly with his kidnappers."

"If there *was* a kidnapping."

The Arlen case was little more than forty-eight hours old, but Matt was already taking heat from above to get it solved. Of course, technically the case was Jonesy's, but from the minute the victim had been identified as Phil Arlen, Matt had been acting as lead investigator. There was too much hanging on it. The Arlens were important people according to Police Chief Clarence B. Horrall, and the least LAPD could do was get the kidnapping and homicide of their youngest son solved in a timely fashion. Matt was treading carefully. Most of the suspects in young Arlen's murder were wealthy and influential people—a number of them also Arlens—and this was the kind of case that could destroy a promising police career if the officer in charge didn't play his cards exactly right.

"A botched kidnapping isn't a bad cover for a murder," Matt agreed with a wry smile. "Especially if the killer walked away with a hundred thousand dollars."

"Assuming Bob Arlen delivered that ransom money."

"Assuming Bob Arlen didn't knock off his baby brother himself."

"He had plenty of provocation," Jonesy agreed. "From what I can make out there was no love lost between those two. Phil was the apple of the old man's eye, and never did a damn thing to deserve it according to just about everyone who ever knew him."

"Bob Arlen doesn't have much of an alibi. He was supposedly home alone Saturday night while his wife was at the ballet enjoying *The Nutcracker* with two other couples."

Jonesy nodded. "He could have waited outside the club for him. Seems likely big brother could get close to Philip without arousing a lot of suspicion, and even with a bum leg, he's a big, powerful guy."

Matt agreed. "And if the wife did get home and discover Bob gone, she'd lie her head off. That dame's crazy for him. Even the muckrakers admit she didn't marry him for his dough. Not that he has a lot of his own. The old man controls the purse strings."

Jonesy scratched his nose reflectively. "All the same, Bob Arlen doesn't strike me as the kind of guy who would fool around with an antique pistol. If he was going to kill baby brother, my guess is he'd just use his service revolver."

Matt nodded to himself. "You're right. We can't forget about that gun. Who the hell walks around packing an antique pistol?"

"Where would Doyle have got such a thing?"

"Where would anybody?" Matt mulled this over. "The old man, Benedict Arlen, collects antiques and western memorabilia. Find out if he's got a gun collection."

Jonesy's eyes brightened. "Now you're talking!"

"Uh-huh. The real question is where is that gat now? If we could find it—"

Jonesy shook his head. "I'm guessing that gun's buried way down deep in the tar with all those dinosaur bones."

"Even if the pistol did come from a collection belonging to Benedict Arlen, it doesn't exactly narrow our field of suspects. Just about everybody *except* Doyle probably had access to it—Bob Arlen, Claire Arlen and, possibly, Claire's brother Carl Winters."

"Winters is supposed to have a hot temper," Jonesy said. "And there have been rumors for years that some of those fancy books he sells aren't the genuine article."

Matt contemplated Jonesy's homely face. The blackmail angle. They couldn't get away from it. Suppose Phil had known—had proof—that Carl faked the fine, the rare and the antiquarian? "That fancy bookstore Carl Winters owns is full of antiques. Let's bring in Winters," he added. "I wouldn't want him to think we were neglecting his side of the family."

Jonesy nodded, turned to leave the office and paused. "You sure you don't want Doyle followed?"

"I'm sure," Matt said.

In a creative fever, Doyle typed up a story from the standpoint of doomed young Phil Arlen and handed it in to Whitey Whitlock. It wasn't journalism—it was more suitable to *Black Mask* than the *Tribune-Herald*—but Whitlock read it, whistled and offered Doyle one of his rare snaggletoothed smiles.

"Well, it's certainly a new angle," was all he said.

"I thought I'd head over to Griffith Park Observatory and see if I could pick up the trail," Doyle said.

Whitlock considered this and then nodded. Nathan hadn't worked for him long, but he had the kind of track record that inclined Whitlock to give him his head and let him run.

"Thanks," Nathan said, and turned away.

"You all right, Doyle?" Whitlock growled, and Nathan turned back, startled.

"Fine," he said.

Whitlock considered this, not appearing particularly convinced—or particularly concerned—and he turned back to the mountain of paperwork on his desk.

Nathan decided to take his own car to Griffith Park. He kept it garaged and rarely used it as gas was tightly rationed—and tires were even harder to get—but he was thinking he might take a run down to San Diego. Pearl had family there, and anything was worth a try at this point.

Including revisiting the scene of the crime—or one of the scenes.

He didn't expect to discover anything significant at the Griffith Park Observatory and Planetarium, and he was not disappointed. It had changed some since the last time he had visited as a schoolboy on a field trip. Now soldiers were garrisoned in the park, and a large air-raid siren had been set up adjacent to the observatory. Class was being held inside the planetarium for a new crop of navy fliers who needed to learn to navigate by the stars.

Nathan ran upstairs to the east terrace, poked around and found nothing. He stood for a moment staring across the wild hills at the old Hollywood sign, and then he returned downstairs.

Out of ideas, he returned to Pearl's Hill Street rooming house in time to see Sid Szabo leaving it. Szabo carried what appeared to be one of those small women's overnight suitcases. Nathan watched him get into his car—he was alone—and, as Szabo pulled away from the curb, Nathan pulled out after him.

Szabo drove slowly, carefully, clearly having no idea he was being followed. Nathan had no problem tailing him even in the rainy weather. He kept a safe distance, leaving two cars between his Chrysler Highlander and the bright green Oldsmobile.

Szabo turned off onto South Spring Street, pulling into the two-level underground garage of the enormous old Alexandria Hotel. Nathan parked on the street and went inside.

The Alexandria had been built back in 1906, and in its heyday it was the center of Los Angeles social life and the city's crown jewel. But the glory days were gone now and, despite the crystal chandeliers, marble columns and "million dollar carpet," it had a sad, haunted quality to it. It was hard to picture someone like Szabo living there. Nathan would have pegged him for the swankiest, flashiest hotel in town.

The front desk clerk eventually stopped shuffling through mail and greeted him without enthusiasm.

"Sid Szabo?" Nathan inquired.

The clerk sighed, as one much put-upon. "I'll ring him for you, sir."

"Don't bother. I'll just run up and say hello. Third floor?"

"Second floor," the clerk said. "If you think it's really all right…"

He was speaking to the wrought-iron gate of the closing elevator.

Nathan stood in the peeling red velvet hallway outside Szabo's door listening for a few minutes. There wasn't a lot to hear. The murmur of voices, male and female, but that could have been the radio—or another skirt with Szabo.

He knocked and the voices stopped. Footsteps approached, the door opened and Szabo peered out suspiciously.

"What the hell are you doing here?" he said.

Doyle looked down at the brown alligator overnight bag sitting on the floor a few feet from the door. "I was hoping for an interview."

"Some other time." Szabo tried to close the door, and Doyle's foot shot out.

"Just a couple of quick questions."

"I don't have time. And if I did have time, I wouldn't have the inclination." Szabo's eyes narrowed dangerously. "Move your foot or I'll crush it. Don't think I won't."

Nathan withdrew his foot. "You can talk to me or you can talk to the cops."

Szabo sneered, "About what?"

"Among other things, about where Pearl Jarvis is hiding out."

Szabo laughed. "I guess I'll talk to the cops then." He slammed shut the door.

Nathan knocked on the door. It flew open.

"What the hell now?"

"If you should see Pearl, would you ask her to get in touch with me?" He handed Szabo his press card, but the other man made no move to take it.

"She's allergic to reporters," Szabo said.

"It must be catching."

He shook his head disbelievingly. "Why do you want to talk to her?"

"A little bird told me she's got a story worth telling."

Szabo's blue eyes narrowed. "What's it worth?"

"It depends on the story."

Szabo studied him. "Well, if I see her—*if* I see her— I'll let her know."

Doyle went downstairs and parked himself in his car, waiting.

Two rumors persisted about Carl Winters. The prevailing rumor was that the majority of his income came from his romancing of rich widows. Seeing him, Matt had no trouble believing this. Winters was a walking illustration for *Esquire* magazine, from the soles of his black Blucher town shoes to the velvet collar of his Chesterfield. But the rumor that most interested Matt, the rumor that was little more than a whisper, was that Winters faked a number of the rare and valuable old books he sold. So far no one had been willing to actually come forward and press charges, but that was because many of Winters' clients were the kind of collectors willing to not look too closely at a valuable antique's sales history.

"So against your better judgment you allowed your sister to persuade you to drive her to the Las Palmas Club?" Matt asked, continuing their interview.

"Claire is a headstrong girl," Winters said. "She was going to confront Phil with or without me. I thought that my presence would help to keep their encounter...civil."

"And was it a civil encounter?"

"No. Perhaps if that girl had not been there, it might have been different. Perhaps."

"Pearl Jarvis?"

"Yes. Phil had become entangled with this creature. She doesn't sing at the club on weekends, so I'd imagined it was relatively safe allowing Claire to go there. Unfortunately the girl was with a group of her cronies when we arrived. Although they weren't together, I believe her presence egged Phil on."

"Egged him on to do what?"

"To…behave badly."

Matt made a couple of notes, although he knew all this, had heard from a number of witnesses just how badly Phil Arlen had behaved toward his wife. He'd heard plenty also about how Pearl Jarvis had sat at her own table with her own circle of friends smirking and smiling and making little asides until Sid Szabo had taken her by the arm and gently but firmly removed her from the domestic limelight.

"So your brother-in-law declined to accompany your sister home. What happened then?"

"I saw Claire home."

"Just like that?"

"When she realized that the situation was hopeless, that she was playing to a crowd of spectators, Claire naturally wanted to leave. She felt humiliated."

"You're a man of the world. Do you think your brother-in-law was having an affair with the Jarvis woman?"

"Yes."

"Does your sister own a gun?"

"No, of course not. Claire is terrified of guns."

"Did Arlen own a gun?"

"I don't believe so. I don't believe Claire would have permitted a gun in their home."

It seemed to Matt that Claire had had to put up with a number of things from Arlen that she might not have been expected to permit.

"Do you own a gun, Mr. Winters?"

Winters hesitated. "I'm a member of the North Valley Hunt Club. I own a rifle."

Matt had heard a few things about the North Valley Hunt Club. Fox hunting in Los Angeles. During wartime no less. *Christ almighty.* "No handguns?" Matt asked politely.

"No."

"Any antique or replica weapons?"

"No." Winters looked puzzled. "I own a pair of Civil War sabers."

"Were you fond of your late brother-in-law?"

Carl Winters sighed, as though he had known this question was inevitable. "Not particularly. I didn't kill him, though."

The phone on Matt's desk rang. He picked it up. Jonesy said, "Is Winters still with you? I think we found the murder weapon. A Remington Rider Single Shot Derringer pistol. It was hidden in a large Ming vase in the back of his shop."

Matt's eyes went to Carl Winters' bland handsome face. "Is that so?" he said noncommittally.

"There's a hitch, Loot," Jonesy said. "According to the salesgirl, just about everyone and his brother has been through this shop since Sunday night. Mrs. Robert Arlen was here Christmas shopping yesterday, Claire Arlen stopped by on her way to lunch with her brother, Robert Arlen was here this morning to pick up a book. Sounds to me like anyone could have planted it—including your pal. He was here early Tuesday afternoon."

"My pal?" Matt asked carefully.

"The reporter," Jonesy said. "Nathan Doyle."

CHAPTER FIVE

$\mathbf{P}$earl scrambled out of her cab before it stopped. She darted across the shining wet sidewalk, past the sculptured-fish fountains, spumes of white shooting into the dusk, and disappeared through the side entrance of Union Station. Nathan swore, finally found a parking slot and turned the engine off. He jumped out of the car and loped across the wet and oily lot, following Pearl as he'd been following her since the moment she sneaked out of Sid Szabo's apartment building and into a waiting taxi.

Inside Union Station was a madhouse. Porters hustled, families greeted and friends good-byed, the sheer volume of sound rising from the marble floors and Spanish tiles, soaring up and disappearing into the cathedral-high ceiling and the gigantic iron chandeliers. Nathan scanned the milling crowd for Pearl's hat—a silly little fur doughnut balancing on Pearl's silly little platinum head. But there was no sign of either the hat or Pearl as he avoided small children, animal carriers and stacks of luggage, pushing his way through the mob of holiday travelers and GIs.

In answer to his urgent question, the gateman jerked his thumb toward the wide entrance leading to the tracks.

There were several trains at the platform, but only one was starting to move.

Nathan ran, swinging himself up the steps as the train began to pick up speed. It took him a few seconds to catch his breath. He mopped his face on his rain-damp coat and then set out to find Pearl in the crowded coaches.

He strode through four coaches filled with merry travelers—but no Pearl. He pushed open the door to the dining car. That was packed too, and he almost missed her, wedged in between a steamy window and a fat lady in a bright blue coat. Pearl was mostly hidden behind an open menu, but he spied the fur doughnut dipping drunkenly over the menu.

A steward came forward and Nathan let himself be led to a table, politely insisting on one with a good view of his quarry.

If he'd suspected Pearl knew she was being followed, he was soon reassured. She scanned the menu leisurely, put it down and smiled discouragingly at the friendly overtures of the fat lady.

All at once Nathan was very tired. His side was hurting from his sprint to catch the train. He picked up a menu, glanced it over. He wasn't hungry—he was rarely hungry these days, but hc had to keep his energy level up. He watched Pearl over the top of his menu.

She stared determinedly out the window at the sky turning indigo, and the fat lady eventually gave up and devoted her earnest attention to a fashion magazine no doubt full of clothes she would never be able to wear.

The steward came and Nathan ordered a sandwich and a glass of milk. He ate with half an eye on Pearl and half an eye on the rest of the passengers. The sky changed from indigo to purple, Pearl finished her meal and squeezed—with great difficulty—around the cooperative but ungainly lady in blue.

Doyle drained his milk glass, waited a few moments and followed her out to the last car. It was a smoker car, about half-full with passengers. He took the seat across from her, lit up and stared out the window. Pearl's reflection took out a little jeweled cigarette case, selected a cigarette and tapped it on the case. Her gaze fell on Doyle.

He glanced over as though only noticing her. "May I?" he said, pulling his lighter out.

She nodded, leaning toward him, watching him from beneath the foolish hat.

"Thanks."

He nodded politely, snapped his lighter closed and returned to watching her in the darkened window. She studied him appraisingly.

"Say," she said. "Have we met?"

Doyle turned back to her. Cocked his head. "I'm not sure." He offered her his best smile. She smiled back. They always did. He looked unthreatening, like—he had been told by a slightly inebriated starlet—a gentleman.

The conductor was working his way slowly down the aisle, asking for tickets. A gabby old guy stopping to shoot the breeze with just about every passenger.

"I'm sure I've seen you around. You live in Los Angeles?" She pronounced it "Los Angle-less."

"That's right." He expelled a stream of smoke as she worked it out.

"You ever come around to the Las Palmas Club?"

He widened his eyes. "Hey. You're her! The songbird."

She laughed, delighted. Preened a little.

"Nice job you do on that 'I'm Getting Sentimental Over You' number," Nathan told her and listened to her warble on about the rest of her repertoire—and then who she was going to be auditioning for next summer. He let her run 'til she was out of steam, and then he said, "I was at the club on Saturday night. The night the Arlen kid was nabbed."

Her smile slipped. She stared down at her cigarette. "Oh."

"Shame about that."

"Yes."

"So where are you headed?"

She relaxed. "Little Fawn Lodge. Not far from Indian Falls."

He had a vague idea Indian Falls was located somewhere in the Sierra Nevada Mountains. He mimed surprise, and it wasn't hard. "There's a coincidence. That's where I'm headed."

"You're kidding!" There was something funny in her face. "But…the ski resorts are all pretty much closed since the war."

"Well, you see," Nathan confided, "I'm not a skier, I'm a writer."

"A writer," Pearl repeated slowly. She was watching him with narrow eyes. "What kind of writer?"

"Screenwriter. For the pictures." He figured that would impress her, but she remained wary. He'd misstepped, miscalculated either her paranoia or his own recognizability.

"You're kidding."

He shook his head. "I needed to get out of town. Needed some peace and quiet so I could work. Thought of the lodge."

"You'll get plenty of that." She gave him that same discouraging smile she'd given the fat lady. "Well, it's been swell shootin' the breeze." She jabbed her cigarette out, nodded to Nathan, rose and started down the aisle.

"See you around," Doyle said to her back. She didn't respond.

Damn.

"Tickets please," said the conductor, reaching Nathan at last.

"I'll need to buy one from you," Nathan said, pulling out his wallet. "I'm going to Little Fawn Lodge."

The conductor drew the ticket pad from his pocket. "Didn't think it was open. Most of the resorts are closed now. Hope you made reservations. It's not weather to be sleeping out in." He disconnected a strip from the ticket pad, punched it and handed it to Nathan. "Train stops at Indian Falls. You'll have to hire a car."

"That's all right," Nathan said, hoping it was. He didn't kid himself he was up to spending the night in freezing temperatures. He paid for the ticket, considering his finances. He hadn't started the day planning on a ski resort holiday.

The train continued on its way through the deepening darkness. He stared out the window. The black-plum sky had a luminous quality that made the trees and mountains stand out in stark relief.

The wheels of the train clackety-clacked along the rails in soothing monotony. Every so often the whistle blew, sounding through the night, echoing through the pines and slopes.

Now what? He'd found Pearl Jarvis—and the fact that she was trying so hard to avoid being found surely meant she knew something worth knowing—something that might help his own position.

He wondered if Lieutenant Spain would think he was trying to skip town.

"But you've got your man," Tara protested. "You found the murder weapon in Carl Winters' bookstore. Why haven't you arrested him? Why are you asking so many questions about Nathan?"

Matt shrugged. "You sweet on Doyle?"

"Sweet on him?" Tara flushed and then laughed. "We're just pals." She cast Matt a shrewd look. "Would you care if I was?"

"Marriage could do Doyle a world of good."

"What would it do for me?"

Matt grinned at her expression. "Might do you a world of good too, Tara. Take the edges off you."

"The edges!" She tossed her glossy black curls. "Thanks very much." She contemplated Matt. "You ever going to remarry, Mathew?"

He shook his head regretfully.

She sighed. "I could have gone for Nathan, but he's…"

"He's…?"

"I don't know. Destined for the priesthood or something, I guess." She grinned. "Now I've shocked you, a big tough policeman like you, Lieutenant Spain." She played with her chopsticks. They were having lunch at the Hong Kong Café. "So what did you want to know about Doyle?"

"You said you didn't know him before he went overseas?"

She shook her head. "He didn't work here. He moved to San Francisco right out of college. That's what I heard."

"How's he get along with the other newshounds?"

"He keeps pretty much to himself." She met Matt's gaze. "He's liked. He's good." She grimaced. "He's bored."

"Wants to be back on the front lines?"

She nodded, took out a cigarette. Matt leaned forward to light it. Looking into her dark eyes, he saw instead a pair of light ones, blue-gray eyes with gold-tipped lashes—direct and yet somehow a little shy.

"Why haven't you arrested Carl Winters?" Tara asked. "Off the record."

"Off the record?" He raised skeptical brows, but when she nodded, he said, "That gun came from Benedict Arlen's antique gun collection. The way we figure it, any one of a number of people had access to it."

"Including Phil Arlen?"

She was a smart cookie; he'd always thought so. He could see that sharp brain of hers ticking over. "That's right. And all but one of those same people had opportunity to stash the gat at Winters' bookstore."

"Let me ask you something," she said.

Matt nodded.

"Is Nathan a suspect?"

"He was with Arlen the night he was kidnapped. What kind of a cop would I be if I didn't include him in my list of suspects?"

"Very diplomatic," she said dryly. She sipped some tea from a little porcelain cup. "Nathan wouldn't have access to Benedict Arlen's gun collection." She followed her own line of reasoning. "But he could have got the gun from the Arlen kid, assuming the Arlen kid was carrying it that night, and that Mrs. Arlen hadn't swiped it to shoot him with it."

"It's a possibility."

"Which is? Nathan grabbing the gun from Phil Arlen or Claire Arlen plugging her no-good wastrel husband?"

"Take your choice."

"Well," she said shortly, "I choose not to think Nathan's a murderer."

She was definitely sweet on Doyle.

She said, "Anyway, why would Phil Arlen have taken the gun? I don't think he planned on committing suicide."

"Well, for one thing, it's a very rare piece. Worth a lot of money. There were only two hundred of those Derringer Riders ever made. And the Arlen kid was running low on dough. He'd racked up some sizable gambling debts at the Las Palmas Club, and his old man had cut off his allowance in the hopes of getting him to straighten up."

"You think he planned on trading the gun for his gambling chits?"

Matt shrugged.

"What possible motive could Nathan have for wanting Phil Arlen dead?"

"I don't know. What's his financial situation?"

She said dryly, "I don't think Nathan thinks a lot about money. And if he killed somebody by accident, I don't think he'd try and fix it up to look like a kidnapping." She puffed thoughtfully on her cigarette. "Any line on Pearl Jarvis?"

"We're still looking for her."

"*Cherchez la femme,*" Tara remarked.

"That's what everybody says," Matt replied.

"**D**id it work?" Jonesy asked when Matt climbed into the car after Tara walked away down the busy street.

"I don't know," Matt admitted. "She likes Doyle a lot. I don't know that she'll use anything that throws suspicion on him."

"She's a newshound, she'd sell her granny for an exclusive," Jonesy said.

"Cynic."

"You think she'll quote you, Loot?"

"I hope not."

Jonesy chuckled at Matt's tone. "You want her to do the dirty work. You figure in her efforts to prove her sweetheart Doyle innocent, she'll speculate in print on all the things we can't."

"Yep."

"You think it's occurred to her to wonder why there was so much time between when the ransom was paid and when the Arlen kid was supposed to be released?"

Matt said, "If it hasn't yet, it will."

Jonesy said slowly, "Whoever did that killing was as cold as Christmas. They shot the kid, and then threw him in the tar pit to try and conceal the fact. Maybe they didn't want anyone to know he was dead. Maybe there was another reason, but I've got a feeling it's going to take more than little Miss Tara Renee asking pointed questions in the *Examiner* to shake that killer's nerve."

The train wheels rumbled along the track. Nathan closed his eyes, putting his head back. He had learned to snatch sleep where he could find it, and this seemed to be a safe enough place for a catnap...

A German flare arched high into the night. Machine guns and 40 mm guns opened up, firing from across the dunes, slicing the night with yellow, green, blue and red tracers—pretty, like fireworks. Tongues of colored flame licking out, licking hungrily for the transports high overhead, knocking them out of the sky. He watched them go down, burning. He turned his head and Matt was standing next to him, watching him. Matt's face was shadowed by the fire, little pinpoints of flame in his pupils.

"Where there's smoke," he said, and he smiled that smile that made him look younger and almost affectionate.

Nathan started awake to a surge of new passengers coming down the aisle, taking the seats around him. He sat up, automatically reaching to straighten his tie, and realized the train had stopped. Turning to the window, he peered out, trying to see which station it was. Old-fashioned Christmas lights hung from the station pavilion. Several lights were dead, like missing teeth in a wide grin. A peeling sign read *..di.. .all.*

Hoping it wasn't an omen, Nathan rose, steadying himself on the back of a seat, and made his way hastily down the aisle toward the platform. He found his path blocked by two nuns struggling with a mountain of parcels, and, instinctively, he stopped to help them shove their packages out of the way. It only took a minute, but as he reached the platform, he saw a Ford station wagon sedan pull up at the far end of the pavilion. A familiar tan coat and fur hat slipped inside, and the woody glided away.

Nathan swore under his breath, crossed the platform and walked out onto the street. He looked around himself.

Indian Falls was a resort town, but if it hadn't been for the tatty fake-pine garland strung across Main Street, it could have passed for a ghost town. A steady wall of closed shops stood across from the railroad station—a beauty parlor, a pawn shop, a cigar store, a lending library, a Chinese laundry. Nathan peered at his watch. It was eight thirty.

He went back to the now-deserted station and read the sign on the ticket window. Back in One Hour. *Swell.* He stared at the final twinkling lights of the departing train now vanishing into the pine-thick mountains.

Now what?

One thing for sure, it felt cold enough for snow. He shivered and looked up at the starry sky. Not a cloud anywhere. That was the good news. The bad news...

He walked back out to the street. Far down the block he spotted lights. A corner all-night drugstore. He started walking.

It was warm and bright inside the drugstore. It was also mostly deserted. An elderly woman with a Swedish accent pointed him to a public phone, and Nathan dug for change, wondering if the woman took much heat from idiots mistaking her for a Kraut.

It took time and persistence, but at last he reached LAPD Headquarters, and, to his surprise, with a little more persistence he actually got through to Lt. Mathew Spain.

"Spain here," he answered, still crisp and efficient at eight thirty—no, nine o'clock—at night. Spain worked late for a married man, but that was Homicide.

"It's Nathan Doyle," Nathan said.

There was a funny pause, and then Spain said, "What can I do for you, Mr. Doyle?"

"I've located Pearl Jarvis. She's staying at Little Fawn Lodge up near Indian Falls. It's in the Sierra Nevadas."

"I know where Indian Falls is. I used to camp there," Spain said, sounding almost human. "How'd you find her?"

"I followed her from Los Angeles."

"By car or train?"

Doyle couldn't see why it mattered, but that was a cop for you. They liked all the i's dotted and the t's crossed. No loose ends. Not so different from a good reporter, really.

"By train. I'm in Indian Falls right now, trying to get a ride up to the lodge."

"Why are you telling me this?" Spain asked, and his voice was back to its normal brisk and impersonal tone. "You're unusually cooperative for a newsman."

"Because—" Nathan changed his mind and took a chance on the truth. "I want you to hurry up and solve this thing."

Spain asked smoothly, "Any particular reason? Or are you just a concerned citizen, Mr. Doyle?"

"I…think you know my reason," Nathan said very quietly, although there was no one to overhear him, no one at all in the drugstore now except for him and the little old lady with apple-red cheeks and hair as white as powdered sugar.

There was another surprised silence on the other end of the phone.

Then Spain said, "You're heading up to the lodge, you said?"

"If I can hire a car."

"Try not to spook her."

Nathan snorted. "Tell it to your granny," he advised, and Spain chuckled.

"I'll be seeing you," he said, and rang off.

Nathan replaced the phone on the hook and approached the grandmotherly-looking lady behind the counter.

Twenty minutes later he was on his way to Little Fawn Lake in a battered pickup truck driven by Mrs. Svensson's grandson, a big blond man with a hook in place of his left hand.

"Where'd you stop that packet?" Doyle asked as they left the silent streets of Indian Falls behind, winding slowly up through the mountain roads. Giant pines and incense cedars blocked the waning moon.

Svensson didn't look at him, pushing the car into first gear with the hook as the car began to climb. "What's that?"

"Where'd you lose the arm?"

"Bombing run over Wilhelmshaven." Svensson looked at him.

If you were of eligible age and not in the service, there had to be a damn good explanation, and Doyle made his excuses. "Reporter. I was in Tunisia with the Brits. The Eighth Army." He wasn't ashamed of being a journalist, but by the end of his stint he'd begun to feel strange about recording and observing the free world's struggle for survival without taking part in it himself.

"Where'd you get hit?" Svensson asked, and Doyle shot him a surprised look.

"Medenine," he said, and the other man laughed.

"Mina," he explained. "My grandmother. She can always tell. She nursed a lot of boys in the other one. The first one."

"The War to End All Wars," Doyle murmured.

"Yeah. When you think this one's ending?"

Doyle thought it would be another two or three years, but Svensson believed it would be winding up pretty quick now that the Americans were in, and they passed the rest of the trip talking it over.

The highway grew narrower and steeper, seeming to wind up into the stars. One side of the road was thick forest, and the other a sheer drop into darkness. And then they pulled around an S-curve and the lodge was before them— just waiting for Heidi and the goats to show up.

"That's it," Svensson said. "Little Fawn Lake Lodge."

It must have been modeled on one of those Swiss chalets that populated snow globes everywhere. All that was missing was the snow.

A narrow gravel drive lined with foot-high Christmas trees curved under a trellised porte-cochère, and beneath the dead vines and bare bones of the carport was a door bedecked in a giant holly wreath. The drive itself snaked back to the pine-lined highway and disappeared in darkness.

There was no sign of the woody station wagon, but that was no surprise. Pearl had had quite a start on him.

He paid Svensson and thanked him, and went into the lodge thinking of possible explanations for his missing luggage. He'd picked up a toothbrush and a couple of essentials at the drugstore, but it was going to be hard convincing anyone he'd actually planned this excursion.

The front door jangled cheerfully thanks to a bunch of silver bells. Nathan found himself in a warm, cozy lobby with a high ceiling beamed with rough logs. Colorful woven rugs lay on the wooden floor, and cheerful chintz framed the big bay windows. A twelve-feet blue spruce trimmed in old-fashioned handmade ornaments towered next to a fieldstone fireplace at one end of the long room. At the other end were two arched doorways. A sign over one doorway indicated the bar, and the second doorway led to the dining room. A staircase wrapped in evergreen started at the back of the room, climbed six steps and veered off into two separate branches.

There was no one at the reception desk. Copper lamps cast mellow light over vases filled with bayberries and holly. Out-of-date magazines littered tables.

Nathan walked over to the front desk and examined the leather-bound register lying there.

The most recently arrived guest was Doris Brown of San Diego.

It crossed his mind briefly that it was possible she'd given him the slip. She had gotten cagey on the train—what if she had hired a car and gone somewhere else? But according to old Mrs. Svensson, there wasn't anywhere else to go—unless she had stayed at the town's only hotel. *Doris Brown* sounded made up, and Pearl Jarvis was originally from San Diego.

He relaxed for the first time since losing Pearl at the station. She was here. He just needed to find a way to talk to her.

Wandering over to the dining room, he glanced in. A waitress came out of the kitchen and began setting the empty tables; apparently they were done serving nobody for the night and preparing for the next day's nonexistent rush.

"Good evening," a voice said from behind Nathan.

He turned. A thin, pale woman with red hair in a painfully tight bun had materialized in the doorway. He knew her hair was painfully tight from the pinched look on her face. Or maybe it was her shoes. Or maybe she'd gotten a glimpse of herself in the mirror—the red hair clashed horribly with the purple polka-dot dress she wore.

"May I help you?" she asked. "I'm the hotel manageress."

"Hello," Nathan said. "I was hoping to find a room."

"In the dining area?"

"Well, no," he admitted. He gave her his best smile, but she wasn't having any.

"Do you have a reservation?"

Since she would almost certainly know if he did, this seemed unnecessary, but perhaps she was short on amusement up here in the snowless mountains. "I made this trip on impulse," he said.

"You must have. You don't appear to have any luggage."

"There was a mix-up at Union Station."

"I see." She smiled a frigid smile that indicated she saw only too well. "If you'll just follow me."

She turned smartly on heel, and goose-stepped back to the lobby, Nathan trailing.

Planting herself behind the garland-decked desk, she examined the key rack behind her, glanced through the register, peered out at the dark night. If a nail file had been present, she'd have probably done her nails. At last she seemed to recollect Nathan.

"May I ask how long you plan on staying? Or will that depend on impulse as well?"

Nathan wondered if the dearth of hotel guests was totally due to the war.

"Just overnight."

She nodded as though she sincerely doubted it, but pushed the register toward him.

Nathan signed his name.

"I see Doris has already arrived," he said with pleasure. "What room is she in?"

Her eyes rested on him for a long moment. "I'll let the young lady know you've asked after her."

"Ah. Of course."

"I'll see you to your room," the manageress said, in the tone of one planning to lock him in for the night.

"I hate to trouble you—" Nathan began.

"No trouble," she said, not bothering to try and make it convincing. She took a key from the rack behind her.

She escorted Nathan upstairs to a pretty little room with pink-flowered wallpaper and two big windows frothed in dotted Swiss. There was a double bed, two white chests of drawers, a little table and a white rocker with pink satin pillows.

"You share a bath with room number seven. However, there is no guest in room number seven tonight."

"Ah," Nathan said.

The key was handed over with the air of one who had serious misgivings, and the manageress departed with the news that someone would eventually be up to make the bed.

Nathan moved to the nearest window. His room was in the center of the hotel. Two dark, apparently uninhabited wings stretched away to the left and right. The night was cold and crisp and clear. A gray Plymouth sat idling under the porte-cochère, exhaust smoking in the frosty air.

There was a knock on the door and the waitress from the dining room entered to make the bed, which she did quickly.

"Not many guests, I suppose," Nathan remarked.

"It's shaping up all right," she said cheerfully. "We just got two more in for the night. Decided they couldn't drive all the way to Santa Rosa tonight."

Santa Rosa by way of Indian Falls? That was a new one for the mapmakers.

"I forgot to ask downstairs, you don't happen to know which room Doris is in, do you?"

"The blonde lady who arrived this evening?"

"That's right."

"Number fourteen. Right down the hall."

Nathan tipped her and she went out.

He waited a few minutes, poked his head out of his room and made certain the coast was clear. He stepped out into the hall and walked quietly down to number fourteen. The light shone beneath the door. He put his ear against the white wood and listened. Floorboards creaked beneath soft footsteps. Doris/Pearl appeared to be pacing the floor.

He considered trying to talk to her again, but decided to postpone it for now. She appeared to be unsettled, and she was already wary of him. He would have a better chance if she ran into him casually downstairs. And if that didn't work, he'd just have to risk knocking on her bedroom door. Not that Pearl struck him as a girl unused to gentlemen knocking on her boudoir door.

Nathan went downstairs to the bar. There were three empty high-backed booths, a row of tiny tables with checked cloths in front of a long built-in—and also empty—wooden bench, and a bar angled across the rear corner of the room. A boy too young to drink stood behind it.

Nathan perched himself at the bar, studied the wall of bottles in front of him and ordered the VAT 69.

"Quiet around here," he remarked.

"No snow," the kid said, which was a refreshing take.

Nathan drank his drink and waited. No one showed up. He ordered another. He thought how strange it was to be sitting here in warmth and light sipping a liqueur-blended Scotch whisky—one of his favorite Scotch whiskies, at that—while on the other side of the world men were dying by the droves.

"I should probably be closing up," the kid said.

Nathan studied him. In about a year he'd be old enough to draft. "One more for the road?"

The kid nodded, poured him another drink.

Nathan sipped reflectively. He didn't think Pearl Jarvis was the kind of girl who would be very happy sitting by herself in her room all evening, but maybe she was worn out from her trip.

He wondered if Spain would drive up himself, and how long it might take him—assuming he started right away. No more than six hours surely?

Abruptly, Nathan was tired. Why not leave it to Spain? He could go up to his room and grab forty winks—which was about all he could sleep these days.

He paid for his drinks, started to rise and then sat back down as two men entered the taproom. He saw the kid open his mouth to protest, and then give it up. He understood why.

They looked like Tinseltown's idea of hoods—or comic relief. One was bald and burly. The other looked sort of like Harpo Marx, blunt featured with lots of light, fuzzy hair. They sat down at one of the high-backed booths. Nathan caught the eye of the bald-headed man. Nathan nodded politely. The man nodded back.

He seemed vaguely familiar to Nathan. He studied the pair; neither man paid any further attention to him, and yet...the hair prickled at the back of his neck, a feeling that had saved his skin more than once.

The youthful bartender went over to take their drink orders, and Nathan nodded good night to him, and went upstairs, conscious of two pairs of unfriendly eyes pinned to his shoulder blades.

At the top of the stairs he waited, leaning back against the wall, safely hidden by the corner.

And waited.

No one left the bar in pursuit of him, and feeling a little foolish, he moved on toward his room. Then on impulse he continued on to Doris Brown's room. The light had vanished from under her door.

He stood there for a moment, and then he headed quietly along the corridor to his own room.

Locking his door, he slipped off his shoes and jacket, removed his tie and lay down on the bed. He lit a cigarette and stared up at the ceiling, thinking.

After a time he stubbed out the cigarette and got up, stepped back into his shoes, shrugged back into his jacket, put his coat on and let himself out of his room. There was no sign of anyone in the hall. He went to the top of the staircase and looked down. The lobby was empty, but he could hear voices from the bar.

He considered. If he went down the stairs and out through the lobby, they were liable to spot him, and even if they didn't, they could hardly miss the cheerful jingle of bells on the front door. He looked down the hallway to where it angled off into darkness. That hallway had to lead to the closed left wing of the hotel. If there was an outside exit, and there had to be, he could probably get out that way and not be seen.

He moved quickly, quietly down the hall, rounded the corner and kept walking as the light from the main part of the hotel faded behind him. It was a long, long hallway. At the far end was a staircase, also in darkness. He felt his way down it, moving as quickly as he could, one hand holding to the banister. No pine garland here. It smelled dusty and closed up.

On the bottom level he found a door. The knob turned and he walked out into moonlight as bright as phosphorus. The cold was like a punch to his lungs, his breath frosted in night air scented with pines and distant snow. It smelled like Christmas, and an odd pang shot through him as he remembered long-ago holidays.

He stuck close to the building, making his way toward the row of garages about a hundred yards beyond the rear of the hotel. They were arranged in an arc around a cement court, and in the center of the court stood a high pole topped by a blazing light. Apparently there were no worries of attracting enemy aircraft up here.

The door of the fourth garage from the left was slightly ajar.

Nathan's footsteps crunched on gravel as he walked toward the garage, the sound sharp in the night. He dragged open the door. The gray Plymouth gleamed in the artificial light. He tried the car door handle, but it was locked. Suspicious minds, he thought with a faint grin. He cupped his hands funnel-style against the glass window, trying to read the car registration, but it was too dark inside the garage.

Walking round to the front of the car, he eased the hood, propped it up and then felt around 'til he found the distributor cap. He unscrewed it, slipping it into his pocket.

That ought to ensure Pearl didn't disappear in the night with the two heavies from the taproom.

He started back for the hotel, walking briskly. He paused long enough to leave the distributor cap in one of the flower boxes beneath the window of a ground-floor room, and then walked on 'til he came to the side entrance.

He opened the door, stepped quietly inside—and the floor dropped out from under him. He plummeted down into darkness lit with red and white flares, tracers and shell bursts exploding around him.

CHAPTER SIX

It was late when the phone call came through. Matt had been leaving for home—or in the process of leaving—for the past three hours. There was no rush to get back to an empty house, and he was not going back to Pershing Square again. He'd had two nights of that insanity. He wouldn't spend another standing in the darkness, hot and sick and shaking inside with a confused mess of feelings that weren't worth analyzing. That he shouldn't have felt anyway.

With Rachel gone it was like balancing on the edge of a cliff—and all the little wildflowers, the netting of grass and roots that kept the cliff from sliding into the sea below, were gone. It was just Matt standing there looking down, waiting to fall.

Even Rachel's memory, the sweet recollection of all they had built, all they had shared, was no longer strong enough to fight gravity. From the moment he had looked across the wet grass and seen Nathan Doyle standing in the shadow of a stone saber-toothed tiger, something had changed inside him. Something battened down had torn free, like a sail taking its first deep breath of sea air.

It terrified him.

And at the same time it exhilarated him.

Which terrified him all the more.

The phone jangled loudly, and Matt reached for it. He had been thinking about the one thing that tied all the suspects in the Arlen case together—thinking about how far people would go to protect their secrets—thinking— because he couldn't stop thinking about it—about Nathan Doyle's secret. The voice on the other end of the line was Doyle's. He sounded a million miles away, like he was calling from the moon.

"I've located Pearl Jarvis. She's staying at a ski lodge at Little Fawn Lake. Up near Indian Falls."

Indian Falls. He and Rachel had honeymooned there. They had gone camping in the mountains there every year until he was sent overseas and Rachel had got sick.

"You're kidding," Matt said. It occurred to him that he might have seriously miscalculated in not having Doyle followed. If he was wrong about Doyle—but if he was wrong about Doyle, Doyle would probably not be calling him to say he had found Pearl Jarvis. He said calmly, "How'd you find that out?"

"I followed her from Los Angeles."

"By car or train?" He found a pen and began to write, listening to Doyle's voice. It was a quiet voice, level. Doyle kept himself tightly under control; at least, that's what Matt would have thought if he hadn't seen him half-naked in the shadows and moonlight of Pershing Square on Tuesday and Wednesday night.

"By train. I'm in Indian Falls right now, trying to get a ride up to the lodge."

"Why are you telling me this?"

Doyle answered, "Because—" And something changed in his voice; he said simply, "I want you to hurry up and solve this thing."

"Any particular reason? Or are you just a concerned citizen, Mr. Doyle?"

He had to press the phone close to hear that weary "I...think you know my reason."

The honesty of it caught him off guard. Shook him even. He wasn't sure he was ready for it. Wasn't sure he could ever be ready for it, because to admit that he understood what Doyle was saying was to admit to something within himself. Something he wasn't sure he was ready to face.

He said finally, "You're heading up to the lodge, you said?"

"If I can hire a car."

"Try not to spook her."

Doyle snorted. "Tell it to your granny!" And Matt had to laugh at the amused affront.

But after he rang off, after promising to send help, he began to worry a little. He thought that Doyle might easily underestimate the fairer sex, and he thought Pearl Jarvis would not have run if she didn't have friends waiting for her—and that those same friends might be waiting for Doyle, as well.

The effort of trying to open his eyes hurt. Nathan postponed it, taking time to place himself. But he was used to that, the freefall feeling of trying to remember where he was and whether he needed to be on alert—even after months in hospital, he still woke with it.

But he wasn't in hospital now. He was lying on a bed—a cot—and he was cold. He didn't seem to be wearing any shoes. He opened his eyes.

He was in a room he'd never seen. The log ceiling seemed a long way away and a little fuzzy. He tried to focus on it. His head hurt. He didn't feel very well. Granted, he hadn't felt truly well for a long, long time, but he felt worse than usual. Quite a bit worse. And his feet were like ice.

He wasn't supposed to get sick. He didn't have much of an immune system left.

"Gin," someone said.

Nathan turned his head. Two men sat at a small table playing cards by the light of a kerosene lantern. One was balder than Cueball, and the other looked like one of the Marx Brothers. He knew them, though it took him a while to remember where. They had been in the hotel bar.

"You're a goddamn card shark, Lawdie," Harpo said.

Cueball grinned widely—like a shark—displaying a mouthful of gold teeth. "No names," he told the other man and glanced at Nathan. His face changed. "Hey," he said, and he nodded at Nathan.

Harpo looked at Nathan. "Well, well. Sleeping Beauty joins the party."

Nathan sat up. It was a mistake. He sat there for a second or two trying to decide how bad a mistake it was.

"Just stay put, newsie," Lawdie pulled out a Smith & Wesson revolver and showed it to Nathan. "Nobody wants any rough stuff."

"That's good to know," Nathan said, and the other two laughed.

The man who wasn't Lawdie scooped up the spread of cards, shuffled them expertly and began to deal again.

"Can I have my shoes?" Nathan asked. "My feet are cold."

This got another big laugh.

"No," Lawdie informed him. "Ya can't." The other man chuckled.

"Can I at least have my socks?"

"Nope."

"Ah, let him have his socks," Harpo said. "We don't need to literally keep him on ice, do we?" He snickered, but Lawdie wasn't amused.

"You gotta big mouth, Hammer."

"Hey," Hammer protested.

Hammer and Lawdie, Nathan noted wearily. He'd have to remember that in case he got out of there alive. "That much I worked out for myself," he said. "You can't be working for the girl, so who? Sid Szabo?"

It had been a shot in the dark, but the two thugs exchanged looks.

"How long do you plan on holding me for?"

"Depends," Lawdie said.

"You talk a lot," Hammer said to Nathan. "It's not a healthy habit."

He was probably right. Nathan lay back down and closed his eyes. The best thing was to shut up and let them forget about him for a while.

He must have actually dozed off because the next voice seemed unnaturally loud.

"Is he still sleeping?"

Nathan opened his eyes. Lawdie was standing over him, staring down. He blinked up at him tiredly, and then closed his eyes again.

"I told you not to hit him so hard," Hammer said. "You probably killed him."

"Shut up, you!"

"I knew a guy died from getting hit on the head just like that. Walked around talking and played a hand of cards and then went to sleep and never woke up. Mike Murphy. Used to run with—"

"He's just playing possum." Lawdie bent over the cot, breathing heavily. Nathan continued to breathe slowly and evenly.

Lawdie slapped him.

He'd pretty well figured that was coming. Nathan groaned and fluttered his eyelashes, then curled over on his side and pretended to go back to sleep.

"Yep," Hammer said with grim satisfaction. "Just like Mike Murphy. Scrawny little guy like that can't take it. Probably got pneumonia too. I told you. The boss didn't want him killed."

"Will you shut your goddamned mouth up?" Lawdie cried. "He ain't dead. His breathing's fine."

"Look how white his feet are."

"You look at his feet! I'm going to hike up to the hotel."

"You're not going to leave me with a stiff!"

"He's still breathing, fer Chrissake! I'll call the boss and see how long we got to hang on to this geezer."

"What's happening with the car?"

"How the hell should I know? I been sitting here with you. I'll find out once I'm up there."

"We got to get outta here before this guy croaks."

"You planning to walk back to Los Angeles? Just stay here and watch him. I'll be back in an hour."

They continued to bicker back and forth for a time, and then finally Lawdie took himself out, the door opening and slamming shut on a gust of frosty air. Nathan couldn't help the shudder that rippled through his body.

His feet felt like ice. His body felt flushed and feverish. Another shiver shook him.

A few minutes passed. Hammer shuffled and cut cards. Then he muttered, "Christ. Leave me here with a croaker."

Nathan heard the scrape of a chair, footsteps, and Hammer bent over the bed. He touched Nathan's left eye—apparently planning to check his pupils—and Nathan bounded up, head-butting him.

Half-stunned, Hammer crashed back on his tailbone, and Nathan sprang on him. He delivered a couple of fast, efficient chops to Hammer's head, and the big man sagged back and lay still.

Staggering to his feet, Nathan searched quickly for his shoes, but was unable to find them anywhere. He sat for a minute on the chair, feeling sick and faint. His head had hurt like hell before he tried head-butting that moose. He straightened up, eyeing Hammer warily, picked up a chair and approached him.

The big man was breathing in stentorian tones. Nathan nudged him, and his head lolled. Nathan knelt, patting him over and finding his gun, a big old Colt .45, which he appropriated. He scooted around, keeping the Colt trained on Hammer, using his free hand to slip his shoes off, one at a time, and put them on his own feet. They were too big, but they were better than nothing.

He went to the window and stared out. Dusk or dawn? Either way there was no sign of Lawdie in the blur of shadows from the close-clustered pines. He checked his watch. Six thirty. It was either early in the morning or the evening of the following day. He figured it was morning.

Easing open the cabin door, he listened. The wind through the pines made a sound like rushing water. The air was cold and clear. Frost powdered the ground. He stepped outside, shutting the door, and sprinted for the shelter of the trees.

He had no idea where he was, but heading back to the hotel seemed like the only option. He couldn't walk all the way to Indian Falls, and Spain and his boys must surely be at the hotel by now.

Hopefully Pearl was in custody already, and Lawdie would have an unpleasant surprise waiting for him when he arrived.

Sticking to the shelter of trees and bushes, Nathan followed the dirt track that led from the cabin to—he hoped—the main highway. He moved quietly and carefully. Lawdie didn't have much of a head start, and Nathan didn't want to run into him.

Every so often he paused and listened. Every sound in the pristine silence was as loud as a shot. Some distance ahead he heard a scrabble of stones or the snap of a twig. That would be Lawdie, he knew.

A bush smacked him across the face and he had to stop. The pain in his head was getting worse. He dropped to his knees, and quietly threw up at the base of a pine tree. He felt a little better then, and, grabbing for the tree trunk, he pulled himself back to his feet. He rested, listening, trying to place Lawdie ahead of him.

It was getting lighter now.

He walked on and the road opened up onto the highway. A deer stood on the opposite side of the road, motionless.

Nathan bent over, bracing his hands on his thighs and tried to catch his breath. His side throbbed. He had no idea which way to walk. Nothing indicated the direction in which the lodge lay.

The deer crossed the road, hooves clopping, passed Nathan close enough to brush him, and then sprang away into the darkness.

From down the road Nathan spotted a pair of headlights.

Christ. Did he take a chance on this? Lawdie and Hammer had at least one ally at the lodge, and it wasn't necessarily Pearl. With their own car out of commission, someone had given them a lift to the cabin in the woods. He didn't believe they had carried him to it, and someone had to have provided the cabin in the first place.

The car was speeding toward him, headlights sweeping the darkness. A solid black Buick bearing down fast.

Nathan stepped out from cover, and raised his hands.

Tires and pads squealing, the car braked sharply, swerved, corrected and skidded to a halt a few yards ahead of him.

Nathan walked toward it slowly. The front passenger door opened and Lt. Mathew Spain stepped out.

"Well, that was a hell of a chance," he said.

Someone turned a powerful flashlight on Nathan as he shuffled in his oversize shoes toward the car. "Who dares, wins," he quoted breathlessly.

"What the hell happened to you?" Spain was peering at him in the white glare of the flashlight. "You're bleeding."

Nathan touched a hand to the top of his head. Gummy. He spared a glance for his fingers. That was blood all right. "It's a long story." He reached Spain, who had walked a few steps to meet him, and a weird thing happened. His knees gave out and he buckled.

Spain grabbed him, two powerful hands closing on Nathan's biceps. Nathan leaned into Spain's broad chest and closed his eyes.

The next time he came around, someone's hands were on him, trying to pull his clothes off, and he made himself start fighting. It wasn't much of a fight, struggling as he was against the extreme lassitude that gripped him, but he made the effort anyway, and a deep, unexpected voice said, "Take it easy, Doyle. We're trying to help you."

His hands were forced to his chest by someone a lot stronger than he was just now, and he opened his eyes against a painfully bright light.

Bewilderingly, he was lying in a room with pink-flowered wallpaper, and two men were leaning over him, holding him onto a bed. One was a big, rawboned man with a shock of iron-gray hair reminding him painfully of Sergeant Yorkie, who had bought it at El Alamein. The other man was Lt. Mathew Spain.

Spain was watching him with those amber-brown eyes—and Spain's big warm hands were covering his own, holding them still.

Nathan mumbled, "What the hell…?"

Spain nodded to the other man, and they let go of him.

"You pack a wallop for a skinny guy." The older ruefully rubbed his jaw.

Nathan blinked at him, tried to sit up, but it wasn't going well, so it was kind of a relief when Spain pushed him flat again.

"Just relax," Spain said. "You're okay. We're at the lodge. There's a doctor staying here and he says you're supposed to take it easy. You've got concussion."

"I'm fine."

"Yeah, we can see that. But it won't hurt to lie down for an hour."

Actually, it sounded like a swell idea. He let his eyes drift closed. Felt Spain and the other cop tugging at him with careful haste, undoing his belt, unbuttoning his shirt. He was going to tell them it wasn't worth it because he was just closing his eyes for a moment. Or…or maybe an hour… He felt like Rommel's panzers had run him over, backed up and run him over again. He ached from head to toe. Which reminded him…

"What happened to the girl?" he asked, opening his eyes. And then, indignantly, "What happened to my shoes?"

"Pearl blew," Spain said grimly. "During the night. Her aunt drove her to Indian Falls, and she caught a train back to Los Angeles first thing this morning." His mouth quirked in a kind of smile. "Your shoes are still on the loose."

He had a nice smile—nice eyes—and Nathan smiled back at him. It was probably a mistake. He couldn't afford to let his guard down with a cop. Even this cop. Especially this cop, really.

Then Spain's words filtered his concussed brain, and he said, "Pearl's aunt? Who's her aunt?"

"Mrs. Hubbard, the hotel manageress. She says Pearl remembered some urgent business back in town and had to leave right away. Had no idea we were looking for her." Spain reached for the waistband of Nathan's trousers, and Nathan brushed his hand away, sitting up fast—which made his head spin and his stomach do an unpleasant flop.

"Suit yourself," Spain said mildly.

Hands shaking, Nathan climbed out of his trousers— acutely aware of how desperately he wanted Spain's hands on him. It was frightening how much he wanted it. He didn't dare look at the other two in case they saw it in his face.

Dizzy, he turned back to the bed and the older cop had pulled the sheet and blankets back sandwich-style. He awkwardly maneuvered onto the mattress, and Spain caught him by the shoulder and quite easily, gently, slipped him out of his unbuttoned shirt.

And there it was: the longed-for warmth of hands on his bare skin, the strength and gentleness that he craved but could never—would never—find except in fleeting, stolen moments.

He crashed down on the mattress, burying his face in the pillow. There were things he should be asking them, things he should be saying, but he was overwhelmed with guilt and yearning and fear and frustration. His body hurt, but his heart hurt more. And he was too tired and too sore to deal with any of it. He closed his eyes, shutting them out, shutting everything out.

The older cop said something, and Spain answered, both of their voices quiet and far away. The lights went out, and Nathan went out with them.

Chapter Seven

The soothing squeak and creak of a rocker worked its way into his consciousness. Nathan listened to it for a while, lulled by feelings the homely sound beguiled, feelings of safety and peace and well-being.

After a bit he realized that he was awake and that he felt better. His head was no longer killing him, his gut had settled, he was relaxed and warm. He sighed his relief, and the rocker stopped rocking. Floorboards vibrated underfoot, he opened his eyes, and someone was bending over him. Nathan shot upright, dislodging the hand alighting on his brow, and just missing a collision with Lieutenant Spain.

"Jesus," Spain said. "If you ever need a job you could probably find work as a jack-in-the-box."

"Sorry. You…surprised me." He subsided back against the stack of pillows. He wasn't usually this jumpy, but he could hardly tell Spain that it was mostly due to his presence.

"You surprised me too," Spain said. "And you keep surprising me." He sat down on the foot of the shiny pink bedspread and studied Nathan.

Nathan didn't know what to make of that. Spain looked at him with an open directness he found bewildering. If he moved his foot beneath the blankets, he could brush Spain's thigh. His heart sped up at the thought. He was painfully conscious of everything about the other man—his solid muscled warmth, the way Spain smelled of soap and Old Spice, the fine clear texture of his skin, and eyelashes as long and black as a girl's. Nathan liked everything about him. Too much. He searched around for something safe to say. "What happened to Lawdie and Hammer?"

"Hammer? Dewey Hammer?" Spain's mouth curved. "Well, that makes sense. He usually runs with Vince Lawdie. Haven't seen Hammer, but we've got Lawdie on assault and kidnapping." His smile widened into that grin that Nathan liked so much. "We're hoping you're going to be able to substantiate those charges. We were sort of going by your general appearance in the woods, and Lawdie's reaction when we carried you into the lodge."

"You bet," Nathan said. "I'll be happy to press charges. Those assholes cold-cocked me last night. I guess it was last night." He looked past Spain to the sweeps of dotted Swiss framing the windows—and the darkness beyond. "Is it night now?" he asked, astonished.

Spain nodded.

"What are we still doing here?"

"Mostly waiting for you to wake up." Spain didn't seem upset about it, but Nathan couldn't figure it out.

"You all sat around here the entire day waiting for me to wake up?"

For the first time, Spain's man-to-man gaze sheered. "Not all of us. I sent Jonesy and the others back to town this morning with Lawdie. You know who Lawdie works for?"

"I've seen him before. Sid Szabo?"

"Same thing. Nora Noonan. He works at the Las Palmas Club. From what we can make out, their orders were to hold you up here long enough for Pearl to slip."

With a sinking feeling, Nathan asked, "Did your men pick Pearl up in Los Angeles?"

"Either they missed her or she didn't get off the train."

Nathan put a careful hand to his head.

"I know," Spain said grimly, watching him.

Then neither of them spoke.

Spain said, "You and me will have to take the train back. The day after tomorrow."

Noonan's thugs must have really conked him because he just couldn't seem to connect the dots. "The day after tomorrow?"

"Tonight's Christmas Eve."

Nathan let that sink in. *Christmas Eve?* Then he protested, "I don't understand. Why would you—?"

Spain's eyes met Nathan's once more, but there was something funny in his expression. "We didn't want to move you. The doctor said you needed complete rest and quiet."

"The hell with that." And then, slowly, "You could have just left me on my own."

"I didn't want to."

Nathan couldn't seem to tear his gaze away. He wondered if he was still asleep, dreaming maybe. Or maybe what Spain was saying was that Nathan was in custody, that he didn't trust him to come back to Los Angeles on his own.

Or—was Spain setting a trap for him? His heart jerked.

Was there a remote chance that Spain intended what he seemed to be saying with those honey-brown eyes?

"I don't understand," Nathan said at last, huskily, terrified that even this much was giving himself away.

Spain reached over and covered Nathan's hand with the warm strength of his own. "I'm hoping you do."

And after a shocked instant, Nathan turned his hand, intertwining his fingers with Spain. He was almost afraid to look at Spain's face, but when he did, Spain looked as naked and vulnerable as he felt.

He closed his eyes, savoring the hard, calloused strength of Spain's grip. "What about..." With his thumb he traced the gold band on Spain's left hand.

"My wife died last year. Cancer. Not long after I was discharged." Spain said huskily, "Can I tell you about myself?"

Nathan opened his eyes, nodded.

"Feeling this way isn't anything new for me, but... loving Rachel made it easy to ignore." His smile was wry. "Well, maybe not easy, but...I really loved her. We met when we were in high school. I guess she—I guess that's what made the difference."

"That would do it," Nathan said carefully. "You never—?"

"I did. In the service. That's when I realized there were guys just like me. Regular guys, not queers."

Nathan said softly, "They're queers. We're all queers. You think it makes a difference—"

"I do, yeah."

Staring at Spain's earnest expression, Nathan felt an unaccountable desire to cry. And that was funny because if you didn't cry when the Nazis shot you, really what was there left to cry about? Unless it was because they hadn't managed to kill you.

He said, "It doesn't make any difference. If you give in to it—give in to what you're feeling—you're just as vulnerable as someone like me."

Spain's fingers tightened around Nathan's. "That's not what I meant. I don't mean you."

"You do. Even if you don't know you do." But he squeezed Spain back, taking the simple comfort offered by holding hands. He had never held hands with anyone, man or woman.

Spain said, "The Arlen kid was blackmailing you?"

Unexpectedly, Nathan smiled. "I'd have had to pay him in blue stamp rations. No, it happened pretty much the way I told you, except when we left the club that night, Arlen said that if I didn't pay up, he was going to my paper. He'd been hinting around for a bit, and I'd been dodging it, but when he left the club he gave me an ultimatum. I punched him. Knocked him down. Then I walked away. The next time I saw him was at the tar pits."

"How did the kid know about you?"

Nathan didn't look away. "I'm not always as careful as I should be. Since I came home—it's hard. There's not as much to distract me." Spain's face gave nothing away, but Nathan knew how he must see it. Facing disgrace and jail—or maybe a nut house—it wasn't hard to believe that Nathan might kill to protect himself. Not hard at all, considering how warped and desperate he must be to do the things Arlen had seen him do.

He waited for Spain to pull away, withdraw, but he didn't. He kept holding Nathan's hand as he asked, "So the Arlen kid tried to shake you down before?"

"I ran into him a couple of times, but he never hinted he knew anything until a week or so before the Las Palmas Club." Because he hadn't known anything until the night Nathan ran into him at the Biltmore. After that—but he wasn't going to tell Spain that. Wasn't prepared to admit that much.

"How do you figure Pearl Jarvis fits in?" Spain asked.

"I think she knows who killed Phil—unless she killed him herself."

"You have anything to base that on?"

Nathan hesitated. "She's running scared. She's either afraid of being arrested or she thinks she's next on the killer's list."

"And why would she be next? Do you think they were having an affair?"

"I think so. But that wouldn't mark her for murder. Unless the killer is Claire Arlen, in which case I think she'd have started with Pearl. No, I think Pearl was Arlen's business partner. I think she used her connections at the club to find out stuff about people that Arlen could then use to blackmail them."

Spain nodded, as though this confirmed his own thoughts. "I think you're right about the blackmail angle. I know of at least three people in this case who had secrets that some might consider worth committing murder over."

"Carl Winters and the faked antiquities," Doyle said. "Nora Noonan and the Denver murder trial."

Spain's surprise was evident, and Nathan shrugged. "Most secrets aren't as secret as people think."

His own included, he admitted with painful honesty.

"One interesting thing, though. I followed Pearl from Sid Szabo's place. Admittedly, I'm no expert, but I think if he's willing to shield her from the cops during a murder investigation, he must care about her. I can't tell about her. I never paid a lot of attention to either of them."

"She could have more than one beau."

"Yeah." Nathan shifted against the pillows. "Look, Lieutenant, I know how it looks for me, but I didn't kill him."

Spain's eyes crinkled at the corners when he smiled. "You think we'd be sitting here talking if I thought you did?" He looked down at Nathan's hand in his own, looked up and said, "My name is Mathew."

Mathew pulled rank and persuaded the sour-faced manageress to send up a late supper on a tray. The doctor hotel guest came by while they waited, and he examined Nathan again, pronouncing himself satisfied with his progress and recommending another day in bed, which Nathan brushed off firmly.

The cheerful maid from the night of Nathan's arrival brought a couple of extra blankets and a heavy purple bathrobe that had, she informed them, belonged to the late Mr. Hubbard.

"From Mr. Hubbard's cupboard?" Nathan asked, and she giggled, peeking briefly at him sitting up bare-chested in the bed. She set the blankets on the rocker, and Mathew took the robe, handing it to Nathan.

Nathan eyed the blankets and said nothing, but when the door closed behind the maid, Mathew said, "Don't worry. Nobody's going to think anything about this. I'm supposed to keep an eye on you, according to the doctor."

"I'm not worried." He wasn't, but he thought Matt had an unrealistic idea about the way people's minds worked—which was funny for a cop.

Nathan stood up, feeling a little dizzy, and shrugged into the robe. Mr. Hubbard had been a bit shorter and a lot wider. The robe felt soft and smelled new, and perhaps this explained the tight, pinched face of the hotel manageress.

He walked carefully to the window, resting his hands on the sash, staring down at the moonlit landscape. The frost on the ground shimmered with the eerie glow of the salt flats south of the Dorsale mountain range.

They were playing Christmas carols on a phonograph downstairs, the music faint through the wooden floorboards. "I'll Be Home for Christmas." And he was. Sort of.

"He said you appeared to be suffering from a state of severe nervous tension." There was a smile in Mathew's voice. "He saw you racing around outside the hotel on Thursday night. I think that's what decided him."

Nathan chuckled. "Did he happen to see me get clobbered?"

"He missed that installment of your adventures." Mathew's arms slipped around Nathan's torso, warm through the robe. He held him tentatively, and Nathan knew that he could move away, and Mathew would immediately release him, and everything would end here. But it wasn't in him—not even for Mathew's sake. Instead, he reached up and pulled down the window shade, turning in Mathew's arms.

Mathew was a couple of inches taller; Nathan had to look up. Mathew was smiling—mostly with his eyes.

"The lamp will silhouette us," Nathan warned gently.

Mathew's eyes flickered with recognition.

"Let's eat," he said casually, and he let go of Nathan, but then he rested an unexpectedly possessive hand on the small of his back as they moved over to the little table by the wall.

They ate and talked, mostly about the war—their experiences were so different it was almost as though they'd been in two separate wars—and then, inevitably they returned to the subject of Phil Arlen's murder.

Mathew told him that Nathan was Jonesy's candidate for Public Enemy Number One, and although Nathan laughed, secretly it filled him with dread. His life couldn't take much close examination, and he knew only too well the attention that would come his way if he became a prime suspect in the Arlen case.

"Who's your favorite candidate?" he asked Mathew.

"I haven't completely ruled out the possibility that Arlen was kidnapped."

"Anything's possible." Nathan was being polite, and he could tell from Mathew's grin that Mathew knew it.

"If it wasn't a kidnapping, I think Robert Arlen has a pretty strong motive. From everything I've heard, he's worked his tail off for the old man's approval and spent almost his entire life taking the back seat to Phillp—who, by all accounts, isn't fit to black his boots."

"That's true as far as it goes," Nathan said, "but Bob's not the kind of guy who would murder his kid brother. Not even if he didn't like the kid much."

"Is it true the old man forced Philip to marry Claire Winters?"

"Pretty much. Clay Winters was Benedict Arlen's partner in some early business ventures. The Arlens were Claire's godparents, so I think Arlen was trying to kill two birds with one stone—take care of Claire and get Phil on the right track. Claire's been in love with Phil since she was a schoolgirl, don't ask me why."

"What about Robert Arlen? Did the old man arrange his marriage too?"

"No." Nathan smiled at the idea. "No, that was a love match. They're crazy about each other. Ronnie was a navy nurse. She nursed Bob back to health after he cracked his plane up, and they fell in love. I think the old man threatened to disown Bob for a while, but for once Bob stood up to him, and Arlen backed down."

"What's Veronica's background?"

"I don't think it's anything scandalous. Her family comes from some chicken-scratch town in Texas. Poor but honest stock." Nathan's smile was mocking. "One of her grandfathers was supposed to be an Old West gunfighter. In fact, that's probably why Arlen finally acquiesced to the marriage. He's a nut about the old west."

"I noticed." Mathew said slowly, "You were probably too busy tracking Pearl across the state to notice, but we've found the murder weapon." He told Nathan about the Derringer Rider found in Carl Winters' bookstore, and the fact that everyone—including Nathan—had apparently had opportunity to plant the gun there.

"And the gun is definitely from Arlen's collection?"

"No doubt about it. The last time Arlen examined the collection was a month ago, so he wasn't able to narrow down for us when it disappeared or who might have had access to it."

"Maybe he didn't want to narrow it down."

Mathew gave him a funny look but didn't say anything.

When they'd finished eating, they moved over to the bed and lay down side by side, facing each other, studying each other.

Nathan smiled faintly. He thought Mathew had no idea what to do next. He rested his hand against Mathew's face, stroked his bristling jaw. He wanted to kiss him—his belly felt like it was swarming with butterflies at the very thought, but he figured that would be going way too far for Mathew, so he contented himself, brushing his thumb over his full bottom lip.

Mathew caught his hand, held it and leaned forward, kissing Nathan's mouth—soft full lips pressing warmly, firmly against Nathan's—and Nathan realized that maybe he was the one unprepared for this, unready for this. He was shaking when Mathew raised his head.

"You're freezing," Mathew said. "Let's get under the covers."

They sat up, scrambling out of their clothes, pulling back the sheets and blankets, snuggling down into the warmth, rolling quite naturally into each other's arms.

Matt touched the little silver cross Nathan wore about his neck. "Do you always wear this?"

Nathan nodded.

Mathew's fingertips brushed the chain and Nathan's skin and collarbones. He seemed peculiarly gentle. "We've got all night," he whispered. "Why don't you sleep for a while?" He settled Nathan more closely against him, cushioning his body with his own, offering his shoulder as a rest for Nathan's head.

Suddenly Nathan was so tired he could hardly think straight. The temptation of doing just that, of giving in to the forbidden pleasure of sleeping in another man's arms—this man's arms—giving up control, permitting himself to trust for just a little while, was overwhelming. He let his body relax against Mathew's, closed his eyes.

The light was off when he woke much later, the music downstairs was silent, but he could feel that Mathew was awake, feel his erection probing his belly. His own dick was painfully hard, balls aching—what the hell dreams had he been having?

He pushed his hips forward, relieved when Mathew immediately thrust back. They began to rub against each other, skin on skin, the soft pelt of Mathew's chest hair brushing his own chest, teasing his nipples, rough but somehow sweet. Mathew's hands smoothed up and down his spine, and he was whispering hot things into Nathan's ear. Quiet, but not quiet enough—not nearly afraid enough—not realizing how the squeak of bedsprings, the creak of headboard could give them away.

Nathan knew. He bit his lip hard to keep from making any sounds, all the while wishing he could understand those words breathed against his ear.

Mathew came first, Nathan felt that slick hot spill on his belly, and he wriggled frantically, writhing, panting, gritting his jaw to keep from crying out when Mathew's hand closed around his dick, pumping him. Like he knew Nathan needed this. Not quite the right angle, not quite the right grip, but just the touch was enough to bring him off.

Afterward they held each other while their hearts calmed and their breathing evened out.

It was dangerous to feel this happy, but Nathan wouldn't have traded a second of it.

Matt's experience with sex—this kind of sex—was limited. Oh, he'd had plenty of experience with lovemaking, and that was probably why. He had loved Rachel very much. Yet in some bittersweet way, this strange encounter with Nathan Doyle in a remote ski lodge was as momentous as any happening Matt had known—up to and including being born.

In a way it was like being born. Like oxygen when your lungs were burning for air, or cold water when you were dying of thirst.

The rushed and harried encounters of marine barracks and showers, the stolen moments in the dry grasses and steamy jungle of Guadalcanal had nothing to do with this, had no reality against the feel of Nathan's wiry warm strength resting peacefully in his arms. He'd never known anyone like Nathan, and he'd known—lived and nearly died—with a lot of guys. Great guys.

He didn't kid himself that this meant anything much to Nathan, and he hoped he was enough of a realist not to let it mean too much to himself—they weren't starting a romance, for Chrissake—but he was glad that there were still many more hours of darkness, and that they would be staying over tomorrow—and tomorrow night.

Nathan shifted in his sleep, a slight restless movement, and Matt ducked his head, whispering something silly, tightening his grip. Nathan stilled, his breath light and surprisingly sweet against Matt's shoulder.

Nathan was exhausted. Well, he'd had a rough couple of days, and he was the type who lived on his nerves. This breathing space was probably just what he needed. Maybe what Matt needed too—a little distance. From Jonesy, from the press, from Tara Renee, from Police Chief Horrall, from everyone and everything.

Toward dawn Nathan woke and they fucked again, slowly, savoring it. And this time Matt was conscious, painfully and pleasurably conscious, of all the ways Nathan Doyle was different from the last person Mathew had made love to: the broad shoulders and hard planes of his chest instead of delicate neck and pillowy breasts; the jut of his bony, narrow hips and the sleek aggression of his cock instead of the soft reception and safe passageway of rounded belly and silky thighs; the roughness of his strong jaw, the bluntness of masculine features instead of fragile bones and feminine face.

Matt liked his strength and his silent intensity. He liked the way Nathan held his gaze while their dicks scraped and stroked in enjoyable friction. Liked the way Nathan's thin, hard fingers dug into the muscles of Matt's arms. And especially he liked the way Nathan woke up randy and ready, just like himself. No coaxing, no sweet talking necessary. Nathan wanted it every bit as much as Matt.

Sensation rolled through him like a tidal wave, leaving him shaken and gasping. He didn't realize he'd cried out until Nathan moved, covering his mouth. "Shhhhh..."

He opened his eyes, staring into Nathan's, and dizzily, Nathan began to laugh, very softly. And Matt laughed too, tasting Nathan's palm clamped against his lips.

"Merry Christmas," Nathan said softly, taking his hand away.

"Merry Christmas," Matt told him.

They had breakfast in their room, the window wide open and the crackling December air clearing out the smell of sex.

Nathan's suit had been brushed and pressed, his shirt and underwear laundered. The late Mr. Hubbard graciously supplied socks. Matt stared out the window at the pine trees and distant snowy mountains while Nathan dressed. He wanted to watch Nathan. He thought his body was beautiful, but he realized Nathan was self-conscious when he stared at him too long.

After breakfast they went for a walk in the woods, not touching beyond the occasional brush of arms or shoulders, but together nonetheless.

"Why do you suppose the kidnappers scheduled things the way they did?" Nathan asked when they stopped to rest on a fallen log. A meadow lark sang in the chilly sunshine. A lone bee zipped past Matt's ear like a miniature Jap Zero.

"They had to wait until the banks were open on Monday."

"But why was there such a long delay before contacting the Arlens? And then why was there such a long delay between when the ransom was paid and Phil was supposed to be released?"

"Well, that last might have been because they wanted to make sure the police hadn't been notified—assuming the intention from the start wasn't to murder young Arlen."

Nathan shook his head. "It still doesn't make sense to me. It's like...they needed time."

"Well, they would, wouldn't they? What's unusual about that?"

"Why'd they wait so long to let the family know he'd been kidnapped?"

Matt knew the answer to that one. "So they'd have no doubt that he really was missing. Apparently Arlen spent more than an occasional night away from home."

Nathan looked unconvinced. "It seems to me that each stage of the kidnapping was spaced so that there was plenty of time in between for the kidnappers to work on some plan they had."

Matt examined Nathan's serious face. He enjoyed watching him, and he enjoyed listening to him. Liked the way his brain worked, liked the easy back and forth between them, liked *him*. Liked him a lot. Maybe too much. Maybe. But he'd never had this before, this effortless give-and-take of equals, not having to guard what he said, not having to sweeten it or soften it because Nathan wasn't someone frightened by the truth—any truth. He said, "Okay, if he wasn't kidnapped, what happened to him? The coroner says he wasn't killed until Monday night. So the kidnapping wasn't faked to cover a murder."

"Maybe not to cover a murder," Nathan agreed. "But it could have been faked."

Mathew stared. "You think Arlen faked his own kidnapping?"

Nathan continued to gaze out over the meadow. His cheek creased in a faint smile. "It'd be nice to talk to Pearl Jarvis, wouldn't it?"

They were following a trail up one of the hillsides when Matt noticed Nathan had gotten very quiet. He looked over at him, and he was pale, his jaw very tight. One arm was unobtrusively clamped against his side. Matt put his hand on his arm. "Let's stop a minute."

Nathan slid out from under his touch, and Matt said, "There's no one around. Relax."

He was surprised when Nathan bit out, "You seem to be taking this very much in stride." He eased himself down on a flat-topped rock, breathing heavily.

Matt dropped down beside him. "Would you be happier if I wasn't?"

"I'd feel like—hell. Skip it."

"What?"

Nathan didn't reply, leaning forward, resting his forehead in his hands, breathing fast and shallowly.

"Okay?"

Nathan ignored him.

It was hard not to put his arm around those thin shoulders. "Look," he said. "This is new to me. I guess I have a lot to learn, but one thing I have learned is…it's not what I expected. What I was afraid of. You're not—you're what I used to hope—" It was too difficult to put into words. Too embarrassing. He cut that off. "I wasn't raised by Jesuits or anything, but I don't think God makes mistakes."

"No?" From behind his hands, Nathan's voice was bitter. "What about two-headed calves? What about Siamese twins? You think homosexuality is some kind of deliberate flaw in the design?"

"What?"

"Skip it."

Neither of them spoke for a time. A hawk sailed through the blue silence and vanished—along with the lark song. The wind whispered through the pines around them.

At last Nathan said, "I went to a doctor—in London. I wanted help. Wanted to stop feeling like this. Wanted to be normal." He raised his head and his eyes met Matt's. "I thought I wanted it more than anything."

"What happened?"

Nathan's smile was wry. "He said he could help me. I would have to go into a hospital—be committed, actually. They would give me electroshocks and cold baths and eventually I'd get better. But it would probably take years."

Matt could feel the hair on the top of his head prickling. "What—did you agree?"

"I did. But then I chickened out." Nathan's grin was sheepish. "I'd used a false name, but I was terrified he'd find me and lock me up. Luckily we were mobilized a couple of weeks later. I wasn't nearly as frightened of Jerry as I was of the witch doctor."

"An asylum would be about right," Matt said. "Christ, you need a keeper, Doyle."

"It'd be nice." Nathan looked away, but there was something in his funny, almost wistful smile that caught at Mathew's heart.

When they got back to the lodge, they had a drink in the hotel bar with the other guests—there were only a handful, and most of them had been coming to the lodge to celebrate Christmas for years. They were a pleasant enough bunch.

Matt excused himself after a while and commandeered Mrs. Hubbard's office to make a few phone calls.

Nathan finished his drink, made small talk with some of the other guests, and then they all went to eat Christmas dinner served in the dining room. Several tables had been pushed together and covered with red tablecloths. There were candles in polished brass holders and a basket of holly with bright red berries for a centerpiece.

Matt joined them about the time they were all finishing up their soup. He sat across from Nathan in the wide square of tables. Nathan tried hard not to watch Matt too much, but when he wasn't watching Matt he could feel Matt looking at him.

The food was as good as anything before the war—real turkey, stuffing with chestnuts, mashed potatoes and gravy. The yams, corn, green beans and pumpkin for the pie probably came from the hotel victory garden, but Nathan couldn't imagine how they'd managed to come up with the rest of the feast. Hoarded ration books? Black market? He ate more in one go than he could remember consuming in years.

Listening to the others talking about the war, for the first time he was aware of being grateful that he was home and safe—that Matt had made it home safely. And the next time he looked across the linen and candles and met Matt's eyes, he didn't look away, he smiled—and Matt smiled back.

After Christmas dinner they managed to avoid being press-ganged into playing cards, and went upstairs where Matt gave him the bad news that there was still no sign of Pearl. "There's been one development though."

Nathan was resting on the bed. He felt ready to explode from eating too much, but he raised an inquiring head.

"We searched Phil Arlen's apartment and found a wad of five-hundred dollar bills in Claire Arlen's purse."

Nathan dropped his head back on the pillow. He didn't say what he was thinking—that he thought it was a hell of thing the cops were searching women's purses, that none of them had a right to privacy these days.

"She says she doesn't know how the money got there," Matt added.

"Does the money match the ransom money serial numbers?"

"They're checking on that now." And then Matt strolled over to the bed, sat down and stretched out beside Nathan. He yawned widely. "Since we're stuck…"

Nathan shook his head, rose and went to prop a chair beneath the room door.

Matt was already sleeping by the time he got back to the bed.

They napped for a couple of long, peaceful hours, and when they woke they had turkey sandwiches and drinks in the bar with the other guests. They made small talk, sang a few carols when everyone had finally had enough to drink, and then at last it was late enough to retire upstairs, lock the door and turn down the lights. They crawled in between the sheets as though they had been cuddling up together every night for years. For a time they just lay there, breathing quietly, acquainting themselves.

Matt's fingertips brushed the scars on Nathan's side where the bullets had hit him, and Nathan's skin twitched a little. It was Matt's gentleness that he felt in his nerves and bones and blood, although it was nice to be touched, caressed.

"How the hell did you survive this?"

"Just unlucky, I guess."

He was kidding—he thought he was—but Matt raised his head. Nathan couldn't read his expression in the darkness, but he heard his tone. "There are about a hundred thousand guys who'd have given anything to trade places with you."

Nathan grimaced. "I know."

But Matt couldn't let it go. "You know how rare it is to survive getting hit by machine-gun fire?"

"I know."

"Seems to me like that kind of—"

"I know," Nathan said again, and this time he couldn't keep the irritation out of his voice.

When, at last, they began to fuck it was very good and Nathan bit back his desire to ask for more—this was all new for Matt and Nathan didn't want to shock him or scare him off. It would be easy to do. It was clear to him that Matt had more enthusiasm than experience. It didn't matter. He was willing to trade a lot for the pleasure of sleeping in Matt's arms again, and when they had finished, pleasure echoing through him like the last vibrating note of a choir of angels, he turned to Matt and folded close.

Matt's lips pressed against his forehead. Nathan could feel he was smiling.

He'd never slept as well as he had in the past two nights.

On Sunday morning they were driven down to Indian Falls in the hotel station wagon, and they caught the first available train back to Los Angeles. There was no chance for further intimate discussion, so they talked trivialities, and somehow those seemed newly significant.

As the mountains flattened out, and the pine trees gave way to cactus and desert and then houses and gardens, Nathan began to dread the swift approach of Los Angeles.

He could feel Mathew's withdrawal, although each time their eyes met, Mathew smiled fleetingly, and the knowledge of what they had shared was in his eyes.

In Union Station, things happened very quickly, and they were out front on the pavement while the never-ending flood of passengers and friends and family parted around them.

Nathan said, "Can I drop you somewhere?"

"There's a car coming for me," Matt said.

Nathan nodded. He knew he shouldn't ask, already knew what the answer had to be, but he asked anyway. "Will I see you again?"

Matt said brusquely, "I'm not leaving town."

And that pretty much answered Nathan's question. He nodded, turning away, and Matt caught his arm. He immediately let him go, and said quietly, painfully, "It's not that I don't—I'm a cop, Nathan. It's…too dangerous."

Nathan nodded. Smiled. "I know. Nice to have had a taste of…what it could be like. That's more than I ever thought I'd have."

Matt's face twisted as though Nathan had said something terrible, and Nathan wanted to reach out and reassure him that he meant it, meant every word. That he was truly grateful for these few hours, that it was the best Christmas ever. He had no regrets at all, despite the fact that he wished he hadn't woken up this morning, that perfect happiness would have been to have gone to sleep in Matt's arms and never opened his eyes again.

But of course he couldn't say that, and he couldn't reach out. He could never touch Matt again.

Instead he said softly, "Take care of yourself, Mathew."

Chapter Eight

"**H**ow'd you make out?" Jonesy asked, as Matt climbed into the car.

Matt grunted. In his mind's eye he was watching Nathan's long-legged stride across the Union Station parking lot, hat dipped at a rakish angle, apparently not a care in the world. Nathan was fine—so why was Matt's gut knotting in anxiety?

"How's Mr. Doyle?"

"Good as new," Matt replied. "He just needed a couple hours' sleep."

"Didn't do you any harm either," Jonesy said.

"Who are you, my mother?" But Matt grinned. Jonesy had known him since he was in short pants. Then the flicker of curiosity in the older man's eyes caught his attention. "What?"

Jonesy shook his head. "Were you able to get anything out of him?"

"He's not our man."

"No? He's sure as hell hiding something."

"Everybody's hiding something, Jonesy. Even you, I guess."

Jonesy chuckled. "Mebbe so, mebbe so."

"Still no sign of the Jarvis woman?"

"Near as anyone can tell, she stepped onto that train and vanished into thin air."

"Swell," Matt said gloomily. "You're watching her place and the Las Palmas Club?"

"Yep, and we're watching Sid Szabo's apartment, but I don't think she'd be dumb enough to go back there." Jonesy turned south on Alameda, pausing for two jaywalking ladies laden with Christmas parcels. He gave a low whistle, and Matt shook off his preoccupation long enough to notice the women.

Nice-looking women. He realized with something like shock that he was missing Nathan—it was like a pain you couldn't quite put a name to. Maybe it wasn't so strange after spending almost forty-eight hours in each other's company, but he missed the sound of Nathan's voice, and his quiet laugh. He even missed the smell of him.

He shook off the feeling, and said crisply, "Tell me about the dough you found at Claire Arlen's."

Jonesy put the car in motion. "The five hundred dollars she claims she didn't know anything about?" He smiled. "Well, sorry to disappoint you, Loot, but that money didn't match up with the serial numbers on the ransom money."

"So where'd the money come from? Old man Arlen cut the kid off, and I didn't get the feeling Arlen's wife was the thrifty kind."

"She stuck to her story. Said she didn't know anything about the money. Had no idea how it got in her handbag."

Matt's eyes rested on the Christmas garland stretched across the street. Funny how bedraggled Christmas decorations looked the day after Christmas. "Let's bring Carl Winters in again," he said. "In fact, bring Claire in too. Let's have a brother and sister act."

Nathan went home to his apartment, collected the gift he'd bought weeks ago for his mother, and headed over to Glendale and the house he'd grown up in.

His mother must have had a lonely Christmas on her own, although he didn't see how that would be possible what with her church dinners and all her church friends and her church activities, but she hugged him as though she'd never expected to see him again, and there were tears in her eyes when she finally let him go.

There were more tears when she opened his gift, a fuzzy pink cardigan. He felt foolish at the impulse that had prompted him to buy it. She didn't wear fuzzy things or even pink.

"Oh, Ma," he said. She was not an emotional woman, and this rare display of sentiment made him uncomfortable.

She wiped her eyes. "When you didn't come yesterday I thought maybe…maybe something had happened to you."

"Like what?" He felt vaguely alarmed at the way she wasn't meeting his eyes.

But she brushed that quickly aside, insisting that he stay long enough to eat a sandwich and drink a glass of milk. "We had real turkey at the parish Christmas dinner," she told him proudly.

"Good," he said, swallowing a lump of dry bread and dry turkey. She had never been much of a cook—or even much of a sandwich maker, but then neither of those things was required to get into heaven.

He thought of the turkey and stuffing and mashed potatoes at Little Fawn Lodge. It all seemed like a dream now. His eyes fell on the nativity meticulously arranged on the long table behind the sofa. The only time she'd ever slapped him was when she once found him playing with the nativity—he'd had a couple of those handsome hand-carved archangels holding earnest discussion with a couple of the tin reindeer requisitioned from the Christmas tree.

She chattered on about midnight Mass and Father Brennan's sermon, and then she jumped up and brought him a small gift from beneath the fake miniature Christmas tree perched on the dining room table and decorated with tattered ornaments he'd made through his school years.

He put the sandwich aside and took the parcel. She stroked his back as he opened it, and he felt another flare of nervousness. He couldn't remember her ever being so demonstrative since he had been a very small boy.

The present was a pen, a very nice, expensive pen. A Parker Blue Diamond.

"For the novels you're going to write one day." She swallowed hard as though she were ready to start weeping again. And, as he stared at her red-rimmed eyes, he realized she had been afraid that he had killed himself.

"Thanks, Ma," Nathan managed. He stared at the pen, and then he hurried through the rest of his sandwich, telling her that he had to get over to the paper right away.

They were still celebrating at the *Tribune-Herald*. Several bottles of homemade hooch—mulled wine and that sort of thing—were circulating with a couple of trays of Christmas goodies—everything a little less sweet than it used to be because of sugar rationing.

Nathan had a couple of drinks—fortifying himself after the visit to his mother—and spent the next few hours doing a little research and dodging his editor.

"Sid Szabo," he asked at large, remembering that overnight bag Szabo had toted away from Pearl's rooming house. "He any relation to the Szabo Alligator Farm out in Lincoln Heights?"

'There was a bit of debate on this point—a few people holding out for the theory that Sid was more likely to be related to a snake farm if there was one available—and in the end Nathan took his coat and hat and left them still debating.

Supposedly the Szabo Alligator Farm had only been around since the early 1900s, but it could have been from the Stone Age. Nathan parked beneath low-hanging trees in the empty parking lot and entered the park through a long white stucco building with a slim, two-story columned portico. The gift shop—offering baby alligators for sale—and ticket booth were closed, but he climbed over the turnstile and walked along the shaded path, crossing a small wooden bridge over a large dank pond filled with sleeping alligators.

According to the sign out front, there were supposed to be over one thousand alligators and crocodiles, some more than two hundred years old, inhabiting over twenty miniature lakes.

He wondered if the alligators ever climbed out of their swimming holes, and if they were able to scale the slopes leading to the deeply shaded pathways. Stepping on one of those three-hundred-pound babies would be an unpleasant surprise for everyone involved. Glancing over the side of the bridge at the slithering tangle of reptiles, he decided they looked pretty tired; it was probably a little cold for them this time of year. Cold for him too. He missed the warmth of North Africa.

Over the murky scent of wet earth and slimy water, he could smell wood smoke. And through the dense foliage of weeping willows, he could see the twinkle of lights: a farmhouse in the back of the park. He picked up his pace, footsteps sounding dully on yet another little wooden bridge.

It was a creepy place, no doubt about it, and it was hard to picture Pearl Jarvis in her high heels and faux furs trotting along these rustic bridges and uneven dirt trails.

But she was hiding somewhere and, Nathan had to admit, this was a pretty good hideout. Especially off-season.

He came out of the woods, and there was an old house behind a new and sturdy-looking chain-link fence—probably to keep the alligators and crocodiles from paying a social call. Several yards behind the house was a large empty field. Two men stood beside a pickup truck, and they appeared to be digging a deep hole.

Nathan watched them, then he reached over the substantial-looking gate, lifted the bar and let himself in. He closed the gate firmly behind him.

He went up the paved path to the house and knocked.

Nothing happened.

He knocked again. After a time, the door swung open and Pearl Jarvis, in dungarees and a man's sweater, stared back at him. She was holding an old Webley revolver, and it was pointed at his chest.

"You can't hold me," Claire Arlen was protesting for the *n*th time. "I'm an *Arlen*. I'm Philip Arlen's *wife!*"

"Well, you were," Matt replied. "Now you're his widow. We're trying to figure out if that was by accident or design."

The door opened and Carl Winters was ushered in—none too happily—by Jonesy. Jonesy raised his eyebrows at Matt, and Matt said, "Sorry for the inconvenience, Mr. Winters—"

"This is harassment," Winters interrupted furiously. "How many times am I to be subjected to police interrogation? I've answered all your questions. Again and again! I didn't kill my brother-in-law, and the fact that you would drag my sister—his widow—out, when she's ill—"

"It's all right, Carl," Claire said, although she'd been saying pretty much the same thing herself since she had arrived.

"I didn't realize you were ill, Mrs. Arlen," Matt said. She didn't look particularly well, but there could be a number of reasons for that—including guilt.

She said coldly, "I'm expecting a baby. And when Benedict Arlen hears the way you've treated me, and endangered the life of his grandson—"

There was what might be appropriately called a pregnant pause.

Matt fixed his gaze on Claire Arlen with the sensation of having been sucker-punched. He could feel Jonesy's eyes, but he didn't dare look at him. This was a bad oversight on their part. He knew how Jonesy felt, but that couldn't be helped now.

"Congratulations," he said. "Did Phil know about the baby?"

"Of course he knew!"

There was something odd about the way she said that. Matt couldn't put his finger on it. Had Phil known and not been happy about the pregnancy?

But a baby would have improved things with old man Arlen, of that Matt was sure. The first grandkid? The first child of his favorite son? Yeah, that would have softened old Benedict up, probably convinced him to reinstate the black sheep's allowance—or maybe even increase it.

"I guess the family was pretty happy about the news?" he tried.

"I suppose so," she said stiffly.

Huh.

"Why are we here?" Winters demanded. "I can't believe that I and my sister are your only suspects! What about organized crime? The mob? What about that reporter, Doyle? He was there that night. Perhaps he's your kidnapper. Reporters have all kinds of unsavory underworld contacts."

"What would his motive be, Mr. Winters?"

"Phil must have been—well, how should I know? I'm sure Doyle needs money. He's been around asking all kinds of strange questions. Why aren't you questioning him?"

"We have questioned him," Matt said. "Now we're questioning you." He turned to Claire. "Speaking of money, have you had time to remember where you got that five hundred dollars we found in your purse?"

"How is that your business?"

"*I* gave her that money!" Carl Winters was white with fury. "*I* put that money in her handbag on Saturday night. You mean *that's* why you dragged us down here?"

"If that's the case, why didn't you say so?" Matt asked Claire evenly. He was starting to get mad. Why hadn't this obvious explanation been explored? What the hell kind of background checking had Jonesy and his men done that they hadn't uncovered Claire Arlen's pregnancy or the fact that her brother was occasionally financing her household? This was supposed to be Jonesy's case, and Jonesy had as much or more experience as anyone on the squad. Some bad mistakes had been made with this investigation, obvious things had been overlooked.

"I didn't know!" Claire was raging. "I never left the house or looked inside my purse until your apes pointed that money out to me."

"Claire, honey." Winters patted her shoulder awkwardly. "You mustn't get so upset. It's bad for the baby." He turned to Matt. "I slipped that money inside her purse because they were broke, and Phil wasn't capable of taking care of her. He couldn't take care of himself!"

Something wasn't adding up.

"Why didn't your husband's family…if they knew you were going to have a baby?" It was like feeling his way in the dark. He was very much aware of how delicate this situation was, and that his own career might be riding on how he handled the next thirty minutes.

Claire flushed. "They didn't know about the baby until Sunday night. I told Phil first, of course. I was hoping…I was giving him a little time to adjust to the idea…before I told Dad. But then when they told me he'd been kidnapped—"

"Wait a minute," Matt said. "Are you telling me the kidnappers didn't call *you?*"

"Why would they call me? I don't have any money. Phil didn't have any money. They called Dad."

The kidnappers had known for a fact that Claire Arlen would be unable to meet their ransom demand. Knew the Arlen family's domestic arrangements so intimately that they had gone straight to the old man right off the bat.

"So you never heard the voice of the woman who called with the ransom demand?"

She shook her head.

The office was silent.

"You think I would have recognized her voice," she said slowly.

Carl Winters was looking from Matt to Claire bewilderedly.

"Let me ask you something," Matt said. "Say your husband wasn't really kidnapped. Say the kidnapping was just an excuse to bump him off. Who would you say had the strongest motive for getting rid of Phil?"

"You can't ask her to answer a question like that!"

"I *am* asking her," Matt said.

Claire said, "Phil's brother, Bob. I guess Bob had plenty of reasons to wish Phil was dead."

Having barely recovered from the last time he was filled full of lead, Nathan was keen not to repeat the experience. And he didn't trust the way Pearl Jarvis held that Webley. Her hand shook, and she had a wild-eyed look.

He said—not moving his gaze from the dead eye of the revolver aimed at his chest, "And here I was afraid it was you they were burying out back."

Amazingly, she laughed. Her voice wobbled a little as she replied, "They're burying Big Al. He was the granddaddy of a lot of these gators. He was two hundred and fifty years old."

"That's a good long life."

"His hide is so tough they can't use it for anything. But they're keeping his head. And his claws."

"Is that so?"

She nodded tightly.

"You found yourself a great little hideout," Nathan said. "That's for sure."

"Hideout? You make me sound like a criminal!" Her eyes narrowed. "I didn't *do* anything wrong."

"Well, I know you didn't kill Phil," Nathan said, "because you're frightened to death of whoever did. You've been running scared since it happened."

The gun wavered, and he reached out and gently redirected her aim away from himself. She lowered her arm, finally taking a step back, letting Nathan into the house. "You're that reporter, Doyle. Sid told me about you. He said you were trying to find me. You followed me to Little Fawn Lodge."

"And Sid's boys followed me."

Her gaze slid away from his. "Sid's just trying to look out for me."

"Who's he trying to protect you from?"

She swallowed hard. "Want a drink?"

"Sure." He followed her into an old-fashioned parlor, pausing on the room's threshold. There were lamps made from alligator feet, stools and chairs upholstered in alligator and crocodile skin, and a mounted alligator head on the wall.

Reading his expression correctly, Pearl said, "Yeah, and you should hear them bellowing at night. The alligators, I mean, not Sid's folks. B flat, I think." She dropped the revolver on the wine cart with a clatter that did nothing for Nathan's nerves and poured two thimblefuls of sherry from a small decanter. She offered a fragile amber glass to Nathan and made a face. "It's all they have here. Funny Sid coming from a family like this!" She swallowed the sherry in a gulp.

Nathan took a mouthful of sweet sherry and controlled a shudder. "You know," he said, "the safest thing for you to do is tell me exactly what you know. Once you've spilled your story there's no incentive for anyone to hurt you."

"You don't think so? You think that wife of his wouldn't like me to pay for stealing Phil from her?"

"Is that what happened?"

She nodded, tears filling her eyes. "We were going away together. We were going to Buenos Aires."

"After Phil's dad paid the ransom."

She stared at him, and Nathan almost laughed.

"Well, nobody can find any trace of these kidnappers before or since Phil was nabbed. You and Phil set it all up, didn't you? So you'd have money to run away together?"

She nodded.

"What happened?"

She gnawed her lip. "Everything went fine. Phil picked up the money at the Observatory. They must have followed our instructions just like we'd planned. He was supposed to meet me in the back of the park. I was waiting in the car. He came hurrying along the path holding a bag, and I remember I turned the engine on, turned the headlights on so he could see. It was so dark and muddy. But a few feet away he stopped and turned around like he heard someone following him. Like someone called his name. And a man came running up the path behind him, and Phil stood there, and he shot him." She stopped and covered her face. "Just like that. Shot him dead."

"What did the man look like?"

She looked up out of her hands, and her face was horror-stricken. "I couldn't tell. Tall, thin. He was wearing a black raincoat and a black hat pulled low. I didn't recognize him, his face was just a pale blur. He fired at me—at the car—and I threw it into reverse and drove away. I should have run him over! But I panicked and I drove away."

Personally, Nathan thought retreat had been Pearl's best bet. Phil's killer had been cold and steady as steel. "You're sure you didn't recognize this man?"

"I didn't get a clear look at him. First Phil was standing between us, and then—" she gulped, "—all I saw was the gun."

CHAPTER NINE

When he heard Nathan's voice on the phone, Matt felt a warm rush. He'd been *wanting* to hear Nathan's voice, missing him, wanting to know that he was okay, wanting to tell him about the problems in the Arlen case. His men had made some serious mistakes in the investigation. *Jonesy* had let him down. Matt's career might be on the line. He wanted to talk to someone he could trust. He wanted to talk to Nathan.

But in the very next instant, that warm rush gave way to chilled alarm. Didn't Nathan understand? Was he that lost to common sense? They hadn't been starting something—those two days at Little Fawn Lodge were all there could be between them, thinking anything else was crazy. Dangerous. They were neither of them the kind of men who wanted to go that route. They had careers, families, responsibilities; they weren't the kind of guys who gave in to that kind of thing. Where was the future in it? There *wasn't* any future in it.

It wasn't logical thinking, it was just Matt's instinctive response to the pleasure he felt at hearing Nathan's voice—because he felt too much pleasure, he knew that much. So he said crisply, "What did you need, Doyle?"

There was a too-long pause, and then Nathan said deliberately, "I'm trying to tell you. I found the Jarvis girl."

Matt's face flamed. He'd been so busy panicking that he hadn't heard a word Nathan had said, and he could hear in Nathan's voice that he knew it.

He didn't know how to back away from his mistake, so he just said, "Where?"

And Nathan told him where, crisply and concisely. "I wouldn't take too long getting here. She thinks she's being tracked by whoever killed the Arlen kid. She's liable to pull another flit."

"We're on our way," Matt said. And then, awkwardly, "Will you be there?"

He wasn't even sure why he'd asked it, but Nathan said, "No. She's got a couple of brawny gamekeepers here to keep her safe, and I've got a story to file."

"Right. Thanks for the tip." He should have hung up, but for some reason he couldn't. He wanted to correct the mistake he'd made when he'd first picked up the phone. He'd realized how stupid he was to think that he and Nathan couldn't be friends, couldn't work together as much as the press and the police could work together. As long as they both understood that it couldn't go any further than that, he wanted to be friends with Nathan. In fact there was only one thing he wanted more. So he said tentatively, "See you around."

And Nathan said shortly, "I'm not leaving town," and hung up.

Several hours later, sometime after midnight, Matt followed Nathan and his newest swain—a big bruiser in a khaki uniform—down the steps of the Biltmore hotel, watched them run across the street and disappear into the jungle of Pershing Square. Matt followed silently, cursing himself—and Nathan—every step of the way.

Who was the unhealthy, neurotic one here? Himself or Nathan? Nathan was at least—assumingly—getting what he wanted out of this. What the hell was Matt getting? Other than ill with jealousy and anger and something too close to despair.

He was the one who'd told Nathan that any kind of relationship between them was impossible. That the risk was too great. The incredible thing to him now was that he had expected—believed—that Nathan would understand that the risk to himself was too great, as well. That he would belatedly exercise wisdom. That he would make the same sacrifice Matt was having to make.

Why not admit it? He had believed that what they had shared was so special that Nathan wouldn't cheapen himself by settling for something else, something less.

But here Nathan was, not even waiting one goddamned night before he was back in the jungle with the other animals.

None of which explained what the hell Matt was doing down here again. And if he hadn't seen Nathan, hadn't tracked him like radar illuminating a target, would he have been trying to find someone of his own to spend a few hours with?

He didn't know.

He was afraid to consider it too closely.

He crept through the grass and brush until he heard them, the harsh panting, crackle of dead leaves and twigs, and he pushed aside the branches and found them—found Nathan down on the ground fighting for his life while his erstwhile lover tried to brain him with a short and solid tree branch.

As Matt watched, the man kicked Nathan, and Nathan cried out and stopped fighting, lying there stunned. The man bent over him. Matt took his gun out, stepped through the branches and hit the guy hard with the butt of his revolver across the back of his head. The man slumped over Nathan's supine body. Matt dragged him off.

He knelt beside Nathan, dragging his boxers up, pushing his flaccid dick inside, possessive and angry about that soft warmth, Nathan unaroused but asking for it—he had asked for it and he had got it—and Matt wanted to kill the other guy. And he wanted to kill Nathan.

"Come on, get up," he told Nathan, locking hands on him, drawing him up, and Nathan staggered to his feet, peered at him and then looked ready to fall again when he saw who his rescuer was.

"Christ, pull yourself together," Matt hissed, and then tried to soften it. "Nathan, come on. We've got to get out of here." He was trying with all his might not to let his anger through because Nathan had been hurt enough for one night. And as angry as he was with Nathan, he was also frightened for him.

Nathan hadn't said a word. Not one word. He reached out to steady himself on a banana tree, and then looked down at the man who had tried to kill him.

Matt collected his coat and hat. He put an arm around Nathan, and Nathan reeled against him and dropped his head in the curve of Matt's neck and shoulder. Matt pressed his cheek to the softness of Nathan's hair. He gave Nathan a moment—he thought he might be crying, but then he realized, no. Nathan was just breathing deeply, exhaustedly, as though he'd run and run to get to this instant, and now there was nowhere else to run.

"Can you walk?" Matt murmured. He had to walk. Matt couldn't carry him, but he asked anyway.

Nathan nodded. He pulled away from Matt and reached for his coat, and almost overbalanced. Matt grabbed him, helping him shrug into the coat, putting his hat on him.

The man on the ground moved, groaned, and Nathan's foot lashed out. He kicked him with the strength and accuracy of a mule and then almost fell over again.

Matt put an arm around him and led him through the trees, keeping to the deepest shadows, Nathan stumbling along like he was drunk or blind.

When they reached the plaza, Nathan straightened up.

"It's better if we don't walk across the square together." His voice was flat.

And that was true. Matt said, "I parked on Seventh Street. Wait for me at the intersection."

He didn't know if Nathan heard him or not. Nathan walked out of the bushes across the pavement, and he stood straight and moved briskly, swiftly, with no sign of what had just happened.

Matt watched him go, gilded in moonlight, crossing the square, and suddenly he couldn't bear it. Couldn't bear for Nathan to have to make this particular journey on his own.

He started after him and caught him up quickly, walking beside him, within arm's distance but not touching, and bitterly damning to hell anyone who watched them and dared to think anything.

They crossed Olive Street and walked north. There was no traffic, no one at all.

And then they were on Seventh Street. Matt took Nathan's arm, ignoring the initial resistance, and guided him along 'til they came to Matt's car. He put Nathan inside, and he was gentle now, careful with him. He slammed the door and went round to his own side, sliding inside. He rested his hands on the steering wheel.

"Are you—how bad is it?"

"I'll live," Nathan said dully.

"He could have killed you. You know that. He could just as easily have bashed your brains out."

Nathan stared out his window, not answering.

Matt started the car engine. He didn't even think about it, he drove straight to his own house, taking Nathan home. He parked in the back, turned off the lights and came around to Nathan's side. Nathan got out slowly, as though he hurt, and Matt put a supporting arm around him. Nathan tried to shrug him off, but Matt wouldn't let go, so instead Nathan walked stiffly, rejecting help without saying a word, making Matt feel silly for that protective arm wrapped around straight shoulders and a ramrod spine.

Up the tidy walk, past the flower beds that Rachel had planted, beneath the trellised carport with roses heavy with perfume even in December. Matt unlocked the side door and put Nathan inside before stepping in himself and turning on the light.

Nathan winced at the light, raising a protective hand.

"You better let me take a look at you," Matt said. "You might have a couple of cracked ribs. He could have ruptured your spleen or your kidneys." He was getting angry again, thinking of it. Nathan could have died there tonight. Died an ugly, pointless death in the underbrush of Pershing Square—and for what?

Nathan lowered his hand, frowning. He said slowly, "You must have followed me. I don't guess you went there for sex."

"I followed you," Matt agreed.

Nathan peered at Matt as though he was viewing him from a distance, as though he was having trouble making him out.

"Can I take a shower?" he asked, abruptly.

Unspeaking, Matt got him towels, showed him the shower. He poured himself a drink while he listened to the water raining down from the bathroom and the resounding silence from within.

Gradually the red glare faded from his brain, his heart slowed back into a normal rhythm. He felt depressed, anxious. Nathan was taking a long time in the shower, probably dreading facing Matt as much as Matt dreaded facing Nathan.

The door opened and Nathan came out, his hair wet, combed back. He had re-dressed in his mud-stained clothes.

And for the life of him Matt couldn't think of a word to say. He was overwhelmingly, abjectly grateful that Nathan was alive, in one piece. The intensity of his feelings overwhelmed him.

But his silence seemed to confirm something for Nathan, whose face grew stiffer and more closed. "I appreciate what you did tonight, but I'm fine. I should be going."

"Drink this." Matt pushed a whisky into his hand.

Nathan hesitated, then he drank. He avoided looking at Matt—looking everywhere but at Matt. He drained his glass, spotted Rachel's photograph on the piano and picked it up, studying it.

"This is her? Rachel?"

Matt nodded. He felt protective of Rachel's picture, prepared for Nathan to say something cruel about her although Nathan had never shown any sign of cruelty. He looked up from Rachel's smile and said, "She looks like she laughed a lot."

Matt's eyes stung. "Yeah. We laughed a lot." He took the photo from Nathan—careful not to look like he didn't trust Nathan with it—studying it. Rachel's photographed face—more glamorous than she'd ever looked in real life— smiled back at him, her eyes shining with love and trust. He looked at Nathan, who was watching him.

He tried to imagine what Rachel would make of this, what she would make of Nathan. Rachel was kind and intuitive. He thought she would have been frightened for Nathan too—and frightened for Matt.

Nathan put his whisky glass down, walking around Matt's living room, as though he were too restless to sit—or expected to be invited to leave shortly. He didn't look at Matt. Matt could have not been there at all.

Matt watched him, telling himself to tread softly, but the words came out harshly anyway. "You know you could be arrested. You keep on the way you're going, you will be."

Nathan had paused at the window, staring through yellow frilled curtains at the garden fenced in white pickets. He nodded, not seeming to notice Matt's aggressive stance.

"If you're not killed first."

At the frustration in Matt's voice, he looked over.

"I know."

"Then why? Why are you taking such a chance? You're not stupid. Why are you risking...*everything?*"

Nathan's face changed. Came back to life. "Because I'm not like you! I can't live my life like a goddamn priest. I need...something, even if I can't have some*one.*" He began to cry. It was painful to watch, painful to hear, Nathan fighting it every step of the way, and sobs tearing out of his chest anyway.

"Don't." Matt pulled Nathan into his arms, roughly, overcoming his resistance, holding him fiercely. He could feel sobs racking the thin, hard body, and he kissed his neck, his ear, his hair, any part of him he could find—a tear-streaked cheek, the corner of a wet eye, his trembling mouth. "Don't, Nathan. I love you. Don't cry."

He was shocked to hear his own words, but hearing them he knew them for the truth. He loved Nathan. It didn't make sense, but it was true. From the first minute he'd laid eyes on him.

All the fight went out of Nathan. He went still, then he shook his head, wiped his face on Matt's shoulder, tried to pull away. "No. Don't." He made another attempt to mop his face on his arm. "Don't." He sounded a little calmer.

"It's the truth. I do love you. I can't...bear this. That's God's truth."

"I can't bear it either," Nathan said tiredly. "Let's forget it."

He put Nathan into his bed and lay down with him, wrapping his arms around him and pressing his face against the back of Nathan's head, feeling the softness of his hair against his face. It smelled sweet, like summer, like grass, like Nathan.

Nathan lay unmoving, waiting for something—for Matt to fall asleep perhaps—but then he began to relax... muscle by muscle, nerve by nerve, losing the battle—whatever battle this was—sliding without a word into a deep exhausted sleep.

Matt held him, cradled him and tried to think what the hell they were going to do.

He woke to the feeling of Nathan's taut ass pressing back against hisgroin. His cock stirred and filled, and he opened his eyes. The room was hushed and hazy with the dawn's early light. Nathan's skin was smooth and brown, and the nape of his neck looked vulnerable and boyish, with the glint of silver chain against his skin, and the pale hair. Nathan pushed back against him, and Matt's dick slid along the crevice between his firm buttocks.

He said, "You can't want this...after last night."

Nathan said, staring forward, "I need it. Need it more than ever now—and I always need it." He added, not in apology exactly, but helplessly, "It makes me feel connected. It makes me feel...alive."

"And it doesn't matter who or how?"

Nathan's head turned. He heaved himself, facing Matt. "It matters. Of course it does. I want it to be with someone I love. With you, Mathew. But if I can't have that, I still have to have it." He met Matt's eyes. "It's a sickness, I know. I wish I could be strong like you and just not need it, but I do." He turned back on his side and pushed himself against Matt's rigid cock, humping back in delicate invitation, weak and wanton. "Please, Mathew," he whispered. "Please."

...someone I love. With you, Mathew...

Matt said, "I—haven't done this before."

And Nathan froze, stopped those tiny urgent movements that were making Matt crazy, rolled over and sat up.

In other circumstances Matt might have laughed at his wide-eyed expression. "No? But I thought…"

"Not this."

"But you want to?"

Matt didn't have to think—he'd already had too much time to think. He nodded, and surprised relief flooded Nathan's face. "Yeah? Sure?"

"I'm sure already," Matt growled.

Nathan grinned. "I was afraid—" He bit off the rest of it. "Do you have some kind of lotion? Or oil?"

"Petroleum jelly in the bathroom. Lie still." Matt rose, went into the bathroom and found the jar. Carrying it back into the bedroom, he swallowed hard at the sight of Nathan lying on his belly, brown and relaxed in the sheets. Matt sat down on the bed.

Nathan turned his head on his arms and watched him. "It feels good," he said. "You'll see."

Matt nodded.

"You're not betraying anyone. It won't…take anything away from her."

Matt smiled faintly. "I know. Now you're thinking too much about it." He unscrewed the lid of the petroleum jelly, handing it to Nathan's reaching hand, watching—unable not to watch—as Nathan scooped a glob of glistening jelly and reached behind himself. Nathan closed his eyes as though even this was somehow pleasurable.

"How do you want me?" he asked, and Matt caught his breath on an unsteady laugh.

"Let's do this," Nathan said after a time, and he sat up, getting on his hands and knees while Matt readied himself. Nathan waited for him, his body relaxed and beautiful.

Matt got behind Nathan, the bed dipping beneath his knees, and his cock was huge as he positioned himself. He took himself in hand and guided himself at the rosebud center of Nathan's ass, prepared for resistance and pain— his own and Nathan's. And there was a moment of resistance, and Nathan breathed, "Yes, please...Matt..."

Matt pushed, felt that ring of muscle give, and then he was enveloped in dark heat—a black-velvet kiss.

Nathan moaned. "Oh, Jesus, Mathew." He sounded broken. Matt held very still and Nathan gasped, "Don't stop. Please..."

Matt thrust once. Felt Nathan's body clench around him—and he began to understand why, once experienced, it might be hard to forget this, why it might even be worth the risk. Was it as sweet on the receiving end? He couldn't tell, Nathan was breathing unevenly, pushing back against him, making that little keening sound.

"Is this what you want?" he asked.

Nathan whispered, "I want you to fuck me, Mathew. I need you to."

And Matt let go, beginning to move inside Nathan, slowly, then faster, lancing in and out, swift and slick, Nathan rocking back against him, begging him for more, urging him to fuck him harder, to take him, to make him feel it in his belly, his chest—naked, shocking, broken phrases that excited Matt more, allowing him to shake off his inhibitions, his fears. He thrust hard, and he enjoyed the roughness of it, the sweet slap of skin on skin, knees brushing knees, thighs against thighs.

He remembered the first time he'd watched Nathan, and he reached beneath his taut abdomen, finding Nathan's rigid cock—Nathan whimpered in a kind of relief—and Matt worked him while he pounded frantically against him.

Nathan came first, biting off a cry as hot sticky wetness filled Matt's hand—it was like he was bringing himself off, he felt Nathan's release as keenly as though it were rippling through his own body—and then exquisite relief was surging through flesh and bone...

He felt tears fill his eyes. He closed his lashes against them, but maybe Nathan heard something in his breathing. He said, troubled, "Are you sorry, Mathew? Do you regret it?"

Matt moved his head negatively against the muscled warmth of Nathan's back.

Nathan kept trying to reassure him. "It doesn't have to mean anything. Not to you. You can forget it, if you'd rather."

Matt listened to Nathan's heartbeat, fast and light like a deer flashing through sunshine and shadow. "Listen, Nathan..."

Nathan was silent, but Matt could feel the immediate tension down his spine.

"I loved Rachel with all my heart. You're right, nothing changes that. But—I never wanted her the way I want you."

Nathan slid out from under him, rolled over. His face was different, grave but sort of lit from within in a way that gave Matt a funny pain in his chest.

"Though I don't know what the hell we're going to do," he admitted.

Nathan slipped an arm around him, lowered his head to Matt's chest. "Maybe the Japs will solve it for us. Maybe they'll drop a bomb on us."

Matt raised his head. Nathan's eyes were closed.

"Don't," he said.

"No? Sorry."

"It should make a difference, Nathan."

Nathan opened his eyes. "It makes all the difference in the world. I mean that." His smile was self-mocking. "It's a long time since I've had anything to lose. I guess I'm scared."

Matt bent his head and found Nathan's mouth. He tasted sweet and sleepy. "Me too," he said. "But I don't regret it."

CHAPTER TEN

When the alarm went off about an hour later, Matt jack-knifed up, hair in his eyes, and Nathan sprang up beside him, pulse hammering in the base of his throat.

"Christ," Mathew said thickly, raking a hand through his hair.

Nathan sat back, watching Mathew carefully. Dawn and all its rosy promises seemed like a lifetime ago. Matt was straightforward. Direct as a bullet, he wasn't going to adapt well to any kind of subterfuge, and Nathan knew then that he wasn't doing him any favors by falling in love with him. Mathew had been a lot safer mourning the gentle ghost of his childhood sweetheart.

They rose and dressed, and neither had a lot to say.

"Did you believe Pearl Jarvis's story?" Mathew asked as they stood eating toast in the sunny kitchen. It seemed to Nathan that Matt kept one eye on the window over the sink all the time, as though he thought someone might be watching them. Maybe Matt's neighbors were the interested kind.

"Didn't you?"

"I did."

"But?"

And Mathew told him about the interview with Claire Arlen and Carl Winters, about Jonesy's carelessness—or forgetfulness—in asking some crucial questions, about the money Carl Winters had given his sister, and about the baby that changed everything—the baby that Pearl Jarvis hadn't known about. That no one had known about until Sunday night, a few hours before the ransom was paid.

It turned out that this was something he could actually do for Matt—just listen to him.

And Nathan listened without moving a muscle as all the pieces fell into place. And it occurred to him that there was one more thing he could do for Matt.

There was a black wreath on the elegant front doors of Benedict Arlen's mansion in Mandeville Canyon, and Nathan remembered that Phil Arlen had been buried that morning.

He was shown through to a formal drawing room. There was a portrait of a smooth-faced woman with two little boys over the fireplace.

The family was busy drowning their sorrows in dignified fashion. They were all there, all formally dressed in black. Claire sat by the fireplace, looking wan. Carl was examining the leather-lined bookshelves; Bob was pouring drinks with the air of a man fulfilling his manifest destiny. Veronica stood a little apart, watching the others as though her season theater tickets were proving a bad investment— that was probably due to the fact that Benedict Arlen was holding center stage. He broke off what he was saying as Nathan was shown into the room.

"Mr. Doyle," Benedict said, and the lack of pleasure in his voice was mirrored in the faces of the rest of the family.

"Nathan," Bob said, uncomfortable and unhappy that Nathan apparently didn't know better than to crash a family funeral. "This isn't the time."

"It's the only time left," Nathan said. "Lieutenant Spain and the police will be here within the hour to make an arrest."

There was general distress at this. Nathan let them work it out of their systems, and then Veronica said steadily, "Who do they plan on arresting?"

"I'm not in their confidence. I can't guarantee that they'll arrest the right person. They might simply arrest the most obvious suspect." He saw her gaze flick to Bob, who merely looked bewildered.

"And I suppose you know who the right person is?" Carl Winters said.

"I think so. Would you like to hear my theory?"

"No," Claire said. "I think someone should throw you out."

"We may as well hear it," Veronica said.

"Yes," Benedict Arlen said. "I want to hear what he has to say."

Bob stared at his father, and then at Nathan. He seemed surprised to find a drink in his hand, and he brought it to his lips, tossing it off in one gulp.

Nathan said, "The police located Pearl Jarvis yesterday. She had an interesting story to tell."

"I don't want to hear it," Claire protested. "Dad, please!"

"Hush, girlie," Benedict Arlen said.

Nathan said slowly, "I guess you could say that Philip's murder was a crime of passion, but not in the ordinary sense. Plenty of people felt passionately about him, all right. Mostly they hated him, and mostly they had good reason."

"How *dare* you!" Claire said.

Nathan ignored her outburst. "And in a way Phil set up his own murder. He faked his own kidnapping so that he'd have the money to run away with his girlfriend to Buenos Aires."

"That's not true!" Claire cried.

"It is, you know. The irony is, if his murderer had understood that he was running away—that it wasn't just another scam, another grift—his death might not have seemed necessary. Maybe *necessary* is the wrong word, because this was more impulse than premeditation."

"What are you trying to say?" Carl Winters demanded.

"Yes, Nathan," Veronica said. "What *are* you trying to say?"

"That someone was clever enough, or shrewd enough, or just watched Phil operate long enough, to see through the kidnapping scheme. I think this person was tired of watching Phil manipulate and use everyone around him, and I think this person was especially tired of seeing Bob Arlen treated like a second-class citizen by his father."

Bob said uncomfortably, "Oh, hogwash. Where do you come up with this stuff, Nathan?"

"Now see here," Benedict Arlen began.

Nathan ignored this too. "And I think the final straw was when this person found out that Claire was going to have a baby. Because that baby meant that Mr. Arlen would reverse his earlier position. He'd reinstate Phil's allowance, he'd try once again to get him to take his rightful place at Arlen Petroleum, he'd shower him with presents and stock bonuses—none of which really changed Bob Arlen's position much, it was more the—the affront of it, I think."

"It's not true!" Claire cried. "None of it is true! He wasn't leaving with her! He wouldn't have, now that the baby was on the way."

"I don't think Phil was ready to be a daddy," Nathan said. "I don't think he had any intention of changing his plans because of this baby. But no one else could know that, except maybe Pearl. Everyone else would assume that Phil would recognize that baby for the ticket back into his father's good graces."

Phil's father said unsteadily, "This is…poppycock. Phil was a good boy. A good son."

No one seemed to have the heart to contradict him.

Bob said stiffly, "Why wouldn't this person…kill Claire and the baby in that case? Even if Phil did leave, the baby would still be a—a rival for my father's affections—and money."

"Because this person didn't hate Claire or the baby. Didn't blame them—maybe even saw them as fellow victims of Phil's ruthless and selfish behavior. Probably thought they—and everyone else—would be better off without Philip."

No one said anything. Nathan moved over to the case against the wall with the miniature display of the Battle of the Little Bighorn. There was a mirror over the case and he could see them all sitting frozen in shock—with one exception. And he knew he was right. And if he was right about that, he figured he was probably right about the rest of it.

"Of course there were other reasons somebody might have wanted Phil out of the way. He had a bad habit of stretching his pocket money by blackmailing his friends and acquaintances—or trying to, anyway—and maybe he knew something about this person's past as well. I don't know. That's speculation, but once I'd worked out that Phil arranged his own kidnapping, I realized I only had to look for people who didn't have alibis on Monday night, and there was only person who didn't have an alibi for Monday night."

Nathan glanced at Bob. "Well, two people. Bob was in the vicinity of Griffith Park when Phil was killed, but his bum leg rules him out as the person who ran after Phil and shot him in front of Pearl."

"I was here," Claire said. "I was here the whole evening, waiting 'til Bob got back with word the ransom had been delivered."

"I know," Nathan said. "You were here with Mr. Arlen. And Carl was at the theater. So that pretty much left only one person." He looked into the mirror over the miniature case and Veronica stood in the doorway, one hand on the light switch, one hand holding a pistol pointed at his back. He took a deep breath, but then the side doors next to him flew open, and Mathew and a number of uniformed cops were rushing into the room.

He glanced back in the mirror in time to see Veronica's hand move on the light switch, and the room plunged into darkness. He saw the reflected flash of muzzle fire, there was a loud bang, and the mirror splintered next to him, tiny shards of glass dusting his face. Screams were followed by the sound of crashing furniture, and he was knocked to the ground hard. There was another shot.

Someone who weighed a ton was lying on top of him, and Matt breathed into his face, "No, you goddamned well *don't*, Nathan. You don't get out that easy!"

And the next minute the lights were on again, and everyone was picking themselves off the floor. No one seemed to be hurt, though Clare was sobbing her fright. Matt got up, dragging Nathan to his feet, hands fastened in Nathan's shirt like he wanted to punch him. His face was furious. He gave Nathan a little push, turning away to where Veronica stood with two police officers holding her arms. There was a gun at her feet. Her black hair spilled loose over her shoulders. She looked as wild as her outlaw grandfather must have.

"Ronnie," Bob gasped.

"W-what is the meaning of this?" That was the old man, looking every one of his years.

Mathew strode over to Ronnie. He said curtly, "Veronica Thompson-Arlen, I'm arresting you for the murder of Philip Arlen..."

"All kinds of things pointed to Ronnie once I started looking," Nathan said. "She was on a bunch of committee boards, including one for the George C. Page Museum."

"The Brea Tar Pits," Mathew said automatically. They were sitting in a small café on Wilshire a few hours after Nathan had nearly got his head blown off playing Master Detective at Benedict Arlen's Mandeville Canyon estate. Nathan was busily rattling off his reasoning, but he didn't fool Matt. Matt knew guilt when he saw it, and knowledge was sitting in his guts like a lump of cold snow.

"She knows how to handle firearms, she's physically strong, cool under fire—"

Mathew said quietly, "Just so we're clear—you ever pull a stunt like that again, I'll kill you myself."

Nathan broke off what he was saying. Color rose in his face. "Look—"

"No, you look. One thing I never figured you for was a coward."

The color faded right out of Nathan's face.

"The entire goddamn world's at war. We might not any of us be here a year from now. You don't think you can hang on long enough to see how it turns out?"

"That's not fair—" Nathan was getting angry now. That was fine by Matt. He'd been mad ever since he opened the door to Benedict Arlen's drawing room in time to see Nathan calmly setting himself up to get shot.

"Don't." Matt cut across, his voice very quiet, and though no one was paying any attention to them, Nathan threw an instinctive look over at the table nearest them. "Don't. Because we both know you'll be lying, and whatever else happens between us, at least let's be honest with each other."

Nathan's jaw tightened. He nodded curtly.

"I didn't look for this. It's the last thing I was looking for, but…I don't regret it. You understand?"

Nathan nodded again.

"I don't know how we're going to work it out. I just know…it's worth working out. It's worth it to me anyway."

"You don't know—"

"Neither do you, Nathan. Neither does anyone. I can tell you what I do know. Love…doesn't happen every day. It doesn't happen at all for some people."

Nathan ducked his head. Mathew watched him fight for control, eyelashes flickering, mouth unsteady. "Don't do this to me," he whispered.

Matt ignored that. "We're, what, three—four days from the New Year? You can focus on the end, or you can focus on the beginning, that's up to you. But I'll tell you what I want. Assuming you decide to hang around and hear it."

Nathan sucked in a sharp breath, nodded. At last he looked up, meeting Matt's eyes.

"I'm not leaving town," he said.

MURDER AT
PIRATE'S COVE

JOSH LANYON

PROLOGUE

The damp night air was bracingly cold and, as always, suffused with the distinct ocean smell. Supposedly that seaside scent came from bacteria digesting dead phytoplankton. Ellery had picked that tidbit up that afternoon from a Tripp Ellis thriller.

The streets were quiet and strangely deserted as he walked back from the pub to the bookstore. His car—well, Great-great-great-aunt Eudora's car, if someone wanted to get technical—was still in the parking lot. Captain's Seat, Great-great-great-aunt Eudora's decrepit mansion, was about a fifteen-minute drive from the village. Walking distance for someone who hadn't been on his feet all day and didn't mind a stroll down a pitch-black country road. None of which described Ellery.

His thoughts were preoccupied as he turned the corner onto the narrow brick street that held the little bookshop that had brought him to Pirate's Cove in the first place.

The tall Victorian buildings cast deep shadows. Most of the storefronts were dark or illuminated only by the faint glow of emergency lights, so he was startled to see the bright yellow oblongs stretching from the tall windows of the Crow's Nest across the gray pavement.

That's weird.

He was positive he had locked the place up after shutting all the lights off. A larger than usual electricity bill was the last thing he wanted.

He sped up, his footsteps echoing down the silent street as he hurried toward the Crow's Nest. He grabbed the doorknob, guiltily recalling that the first words Chief Carson had ever spoken to him concerned replacing the sticky old lock with a new deadbolt. His dismay ratcheted up another notch as the door swung open on well-oiled hinges.

Oh no.

No way had he forgotten to lock up. He had lived in New York most of his life, for heaven's sake. Locking doors was second nature to him. Sure, Pirate's Cove was a small town, but all you had to do was flip through a couple of titles in the cozy-mystery section to know that evil lurked in the cutest, quaintest corners of the universe.

"Hello?" he called.

His uneasy gaze fell on the thing lying just a few feet inside the shop. A purple-plumed tricorn hat. He looked past the hat, and his breath caught. His heart shuddered to a stop.

"No," he whispered. "No way…"

At first glance there appeared to be a drunken pirate passed out on the floor of the Crow's Nest. His disbelieving eyes took in the glossy boots, black velvet breeches, long, plum-colored coat and gold-trimmed vest, the scarlet lace jabot…

Scarlet.

Because the lacy folds were soaked in blood. The same blood slowly spreading around the motionless—terrifyingly motionless—form sprawled on newly sanded hardwood floors.

He put a hand out to steady himself—except there was nothing to grab—so he stumbled forward, landing on his knees beside the body. He instinctively reached to check for… But there was no need. The eerie stillness of the man's chest, the glassy stare, the gray and bloodless face… Trevor Maples was dead. Tiny, twin, horror-stricken reflections of himself in those sightless blue eyes.

He drew back, climbed clumsily to his feet, and staggered out the open door to the uncannily silent street.

"Help!" he cried. "Help! Murder!"

One by one, the street's lamps turned on as residents in the apartments above the shops surrounding the Crow's Nest woke to the cries of death and disaster. The windows of normally sleepy little Pirate's Cove lit up like the stars winking overhead.

CHAPTER ONE

A *few hours earlier…*

Ellery Page was thinking of murder.

Given that he was standing in the middle of a mystery bookstore, maybe that wasn't surprising.

Or maybe it was, since he had never expected to be the owner of a bookstore, mystery or otherwise. However, Ellery was not thinking of fictional murders. He was not thinking of locked-room or impossible mysteries, nor romantic suspense (definitely *not* romantic anything) nor serial-killer thrillers. Nope. He was thinking of picking up the small bronze crow (it was actually a raven, had Great-great-great-aunt Eudora only known) paperweight and conking Trevor Maples over the head.

"Yes or no?" Trevor demanded, oblivious to the tension hanging in the air of the Crow's Nest bookshop. It was the middle of the day, and the sunlight off the ocean filtered through the big bay windows of the corner shop, glancing off the row of ships' lanterns lining the back wall. The light reflecting off the glass, prismed in sea glass flashes of blue and green, created the charming illusion of an undersea grotto.

Well, it wasn't all illusion. Financially speaking, the shop was definitely underwater.

Which was why it made sense to accept Trevor's offer.

"Same answer as before," Ellery replied. "No."

No one had ever accused him of being overly sensible.

"I don't understand you," Trevor protested. "You asked for more money. I've upped my original offer *twice*."

"I *didn't* ask for more money. *You* said I was holding out for more money and that you wouldn't raise your offer."

Trevor's buffed, professionally manicured nails beat impatiently against the wooden counter. *Tap, tap, tap. Tap, tap, tap.* Each time his fingertips hit the counter, Ellery tried not to wince. Trevor was, at least in his own opinion, kind of a big deal in Pirate's Cove. He owned three of the most successful shops in the village and was currently the leading candidate for mayor.

Apparently, the fact that the Crow's Nest had a few dusty first editions for sale put Ellery in direct competition with Gimcrack Antiques, Trevor's most successful business enterprise, but Ellery found that hard to believe. The Crow's Nest had been foundering for a long time. He had to believe there was some other more pressing reason that Trevor was so determined to buy him out. So determined, in fact, that he'd shown up on a Saturday morning, taking time out from his campaigning. This made it his third attempt in as many weeks to buy the Crow's Nest.

"You said the shop held no sentimental value for you. You never even met Eudora. What else *could* you mean besides wanting more money?"

Trevor looked around at the store as he waited for Ellery's answer. His lip curled.

It wasn't hard to read his mind. Great-great-great-aunt Eudora had died in February, and though Ellery had been working steadily for the last three months, trying to get everything shipshape, you couldn't undo forty years of dust and disorganization just like that. To add to the challenge, Great-great-great-aunt Eudora had been quite a hoarder during the last few years of her life. Every time Ellery had to go down to the cellar, he feared he would be crushed beneath one of those teetering towers of moldy paperbacks.

"Well?" Trevor cocked a gingery eyebrow at Ellery. He looked pointedly at his open checkbook.

"Well what?"

"What is it you want, if not money?" *Tap, tap, tap.* Trevor's fingers drummed across the wood a little faster as his impatience grew.

"It's not about money," Ellery said.

Trevor drawled, "It's *always* about money."

And he wasn't completely wrong. The offer of a ready-made home and business had definitely factored into Ellery's decision to leave his life in New York. Timing had also been a consideration. Opportunity had knocked in the form of Great-great-great-aunt Eudora's passing, and Ellery had answered.

Someone behind the tall shelf of espionage and spy thrillers coughed. Ellery hadn't realized there were any customers in the shop. That was a good sign!

"So?" Trevor snapped. "What's it going to be?"

Ellery didn't want to get all expansive with Trevor, but he needed these impromptu visits to stop, and maybe he hadn't been clear enough in their previous conversations. He said, a little apologetically because he did not like confrontation, "The thing is, Mr. Maples, my inheriting this bookstore gave me a chance to start over. I was ready to start fresh, and this is the opportunity I was waiting for. I like Pirate's Cove. I'm getting to love living in a small town. I even sort of enjoy running a bookstore—"

"You don't have to leave Pirate's Cove," Trevor interrupted. "I'm not running you out of town. You can stay in the village. You can even stay on in the bookstore, working for me. I can always use good help, and you've done an impre—decent job of cleaning out this rat's nest and getting the shop up and running."

What an ass.

Ellery said firmly, "I'm sorry, the Crow's Nest is not for sale." His cheeks hurt with the effort of keeping his pleasant smile *up and running.*

Trevor looked as taken aback as if the bronze paperweight had spoken up. His expression hardened. "I see," he said dryly. "Fine. Name your price. I'll pay whatever you want. Within reason, of course."

Did Trevor really think this was all about negotiating for a better deal? Yeah, he probably did, because that was what he would be doing in Ellery's place. Anyway, what the heck was his obsession with taking over the Crow's Nest? Pirate's Cove was surely large enough to support two antiques shops or two bookstores or two anythings. Especially in the summer, when business picked up. That was the rumor, at least. Business picked up when the weather turned warm and the tourists arrived.

Of course, if Trevor's claim that Great-great-great-aunt Eudora had promised to sell to him was true, his frustration with the way things had turned out was understandable. But according to Mr. Landry, Great-great-great-aunt Eudora's lawyer, no such sale had been in the works. In fact, Mr. Landry insisted Great-great-great-aunt Eudora would never have willingly sold to Trevor.

Maybe it would have been different if Trevor wasn't so arrogant, so pushy. His offer was a fair one—and this new offer was likely more than fair—and it was true that Ellery had no sentimental attachment to the shop or to the bookselling business. With the money from the sale of the Crow's Nest he could open another business, maybe even one with a better chance of success. But Trevor was so unpleasant, it made even someone as easygoing as Ellery want to thwart him.

"That's very generous, but no."

Trevor glowered. "Yes, it *is* generous. And it's a limited-time offer."

Ellery shrugged.

"You can't be serious." Trevor's voice rose. "This place is practically falling down around your ears. You don't know the first thing about running a bookstore. And for all your talk about second chances and loving life in a small town, we both know you're not going to stick around for long. You don't belong here."

Wow. Really? Trevor was one step from telling him, *We don't take kindly to your sort around these parts!*

Maybe he was right. Maybe it was true. But as much as Ellery didn't like confrontation, he had a stubborn streak, and the more Trevor insisted he *had* to sell, the more certain Ellery became that no way was he selling to Trevor.

"Sorry. I really don't know what else to tell you. The Crow's Nest is not for sale. Not now. Not ever." *Not to you.* Ellery managed not to say that last aloud, but it was probably in his tone.

Trevor stared at him for a long moment. "We'll see," he said finally. He even smiled. It was not a nice smile. "I'll give you twenty-four hours to change your mind. I suggest you think long and hard about the future. Especially if you're planning on spending it in *my* town."

The threat was hard to miss. Ellery said nothing. He was thinking Trevor was like the villain in a bad movie— maybe a Hallmark movie because there was no physical threat and even the nonphysical threat was vague. Clearly Trevor believed he had the election in the bag.

Snidely Whiplash, a.k.a. Trevor, knew better than to waste a good exit line. He turned and headed for the front entrance. The bell tinkled cheerily as he opened the door, and then again as the door banged shut. The antique cutlass hanging above the frame slipped off one of its hooks, and the blade swung down, slicing through the air in a deadly arc.

About the Author

Author of over ninety titles of classic Male/Male fiction featuring twisty mystery, kickass adventure, and unapologetic man-on-man romance, JOSH LANYON'S work has been translated into twelve languages. Her FBI thriller *Fair Game* was the first Male/Male title to be published by Harlequin Mondadori, then the largest romance publisher in Italy. *Stranger on the Shore* (Harper Collins Italia) was the first M/M title to be published in print. In 2016 *Fatal Shadows* placed #5 in Japan's annual Boy Love novel list (the first and only title by a foreign author to place on the list). The Adrien English series was awarded the All Time Favorite Couple by the Goodreads M/M Romance Group. In 2019, *Fatal Shadows* became the first LGBTQ mobile game created by Moments: Choose Your Story.

She is an Eppie Award winner, a four-time Lambda Literary Award finalist (twice for Gay Mystery), an Edgar nominee, and the first ever recipient of the Goodreads All Time Favorite M/M Author award.

Josh is married and lives in Southern California.

Find other Josh Lanyon titles at www.joshlanyon.com, and follow her on Twitter, Facebook, Goodreads, Instagram and Tumblr.

For extras and other exclusives, please join Josh on Patreon at https://www.patreon.com/joshlanyon.

ALSO BY JOSH LANYON

NOVELS

The ADRIEN ENGLISH Mysteries
Fatal Shadows • A Dangerous Thing • The Hell You Say
Death of a Pirate King • The Dark Tide
So This is Christmas • Stranger Things Have Happened

The HOLMES & MORIARITY Mysteries
Somebody Killed His Editor • All She Wrote
The Boy with the Painful Tattoo • In Other Words...Murder

The ALL'S FAIR Series
Fair Game • Fair Play • Fair Chance

The ART OF MURDER Series
The Mermaid Murders •The Monet Murders
The Magician Murders • The Monuments Men Murders

The SECRETS AND SCRABBLE Series
Murder at Pirate's Cove • Secret at Skull House

OTHER NOVELS
The Ghost Wore Yellow Socks
Mexican Heat (with Laura Baumbach)
Strange Fortune • Come Unto These Yellow Sands
This Rough Magic • Stranger on the Shore • Winter Kill
Murder in Pastel • Jefferson Blythe, Esquire
The Curse of the Blue Scarab • Murder Takes the High Road
Séance on a Summer's Night • The Ghost Had an Early Check-Out

NOVELLAS

The DANGEROUS GROUND Series

*Dangerous Ground • Old Poison • Blood Heat
Dead Run • Kick Start*

The I SPY Series

*I Spy Something Bloody • I Spy Something Wicked
I Spy Something Christmas*

The IN A DARK WOOD Series

In a Dark Wood • The Parting Glass

The DARK HORSE Series

The Dark Horse • The White Knight

The DOYLE & SPAIN Series

Snowball in Hell

The HAUNTED HEART Series

Haunted Heart Winter

The XOXO FILES Series

Mummie Dearest

OTHER NOVELLAS

*Cards on the Table • The Dark Farewell
The Darkling Thrush • The Dickens with Love
Don't Look Back • A Ghost of a Chance
Lovers and Other Strangers • Out of the Blue
A Vintage Affair • Lone Star (in Men Under the Mistletoe)
Green Glass Beads (in Irregulars)
Blood Red Butterfly • Everything I Know
Baby, It's Cold • A Case of Christmas
Murder Between the Pages • Slay Ride*

SHORT STORIES

A Limited Engagement • The French Have a Word for It
In Sunshine or In Shadow • Until We Meet Once More
Icecapade (in His for the Holidays) • Perfect Day
Heart Trouble • In Plain Sight • Wedding Favors
Wizard's Moon • Fade to Black • Night Watch
Plenty of Fish • The Boy Next Door
Halloween is Murder

COLLECTIONS

Stories (Vol. 1) • Sweet Spot (the Petit Morts)
Merry Christmas, Darling (Holiday Codas)
Christmas Waltz (Holiday Codas 2)
I Spy…Three Novellas
Point Blank (Five Dangerous Ground Novellas)
Dark Horse, White Knight (Two Novellas)
The Adrien English Mysteries
The Adrien English Mysteries 2

www.ingramcontent.com/pod-product-compliance
Lightning Source LLC
Chambersburg PA
CBHW070653100726
47907CB00007B/2189